MH

This book should be returned to any branch of the
Lancashire County Library on or before the date shown

CART		AH
2 6 JUL 2019		
27th Nov		
11 DEC 2021		

Lancashire County Library
Bowran Street
Preston PR1 2UX
www.lancashire.gov.uk/libraries

Lancashire
County
Council

D1491472

SLOW DANCE
WITH THE
BEST MAN

SLOW DANCE WITH THE BEST MAN

BY

SOPHIE PEMBROKE

First published in Great Britain 2016
By Mills & Boon, an imprint of HarperCollins*Publishers*
1 London Bridge Street, London, SE1 9GF

Large Print edition 2017

© 2016 Sophie Pembroke

ISBN: 978-0-263-07095-8

Printed and bound in Great Britain
by CPI Antony Rowe, Chippenham, Wiltshire

118148684

For Simon, after ten wonderful years of marriage. Here's to many more. x

CHAPTER ONE

THREE DAYS AFTER CHRISTMAS, Eloise Miller stood on the ancient stone steps of Morwen Hall, her hands clasped over the buttons of her dove-grey wool coat, and waited for her childhood arch nemesis to arrive and all hell to break loose.

'I wonder if she'll wear the veil,' Laurel mused beside her. 'I mean, she sent me scampering all over the country looking for the absolute perfect lace confection, but I can't help thinking that Melissa really doesn't like it when people can't see her face.'

'Which explains those awful billboards for her latest film,' Eloise agreed, thinking of the monstrosities, tall as double decker buses, which featured little more than Melissa's flawless features, shiny blonde hair and slim, pale shoulders. Oh, and the name of the film, probably. But Eloise would bet money that no one who'd seen the posters could remember what the film was called.

Melissa had the sort of captivating beauty that made everything else fade into insignificance. Except the fact she was a perennial mean girl, of course.

'Do you think she's as…demanding on set as she has been over this wedding?' Laurel asked and, not for the first time, Eloise felt a burst of sympathy for her new friend. As Melissa's half-sister *and* wedding planner, Laurel had it far worse than Eloise. Not only did Laurel have to manage a whole five-day wedding celebration extravaganza for the rich and famous but, once this wedding was over, Eloise would never have to see Melissa again. Laurel would.

Mind you, having survived the teenage years, Eloise had been pretty sure that misery at Melissa's hands was over for her, especially once Melissa set sail for Hollywood and stardom. And once she'd actually found it, against all the odds, Eloise had been *certain* that she'd never have to get closer to Melissa Sommers than a movie poster ever again.

That was until Melissa revealed her engagement to A-list Hollywood actor, Riley Black, in *Star!* magazine, wearing a giant rock of a diamond on her left hand, and announced her intention to get married back home in England. And not just England—at Morwen Hall, the elite, luxury Gothic stately home turned hotel where she'd spent her teenage years working as a maid, and making Eloise's life miserable. Well, the last bit wasn't in the magazine, but it was all Eloise had been able to see when her boss had shown her the article.

'She can't possibly be as bad on set,' Eloise answered, shifting from one foot to the other to try and keep warm. She'd go back inside, but she knew the moment she turned her back would be the moment Melissa turned up, complete with her fiancé and his even more famous best man— Noah Cross. That was just the sort of luck she had. And, as the interim manager of Morwen Hall, it was her job to be there to greet their VIP guests. Even if they were planning on filling her hotel with *actors*. 'She's not that good an actress. They wouldn't keep casting her in all those blockbusters if she was as much of a pain to work with as she has been lately. Or as she was at Morwen Hall ten years ago, come to that.'

Laurel turned to look at her, curious. 'What

was she like? I never even met her until she was sixteen, after my dad, well…you know.'

Eloise did know. She suspected most of Britain—the world, even—knew the story of how Melissa Sommers had been brought up by her single mum, her dad visiting only when he could get away from his real family across town. Laurel's family.

'Organising this wedding has been the most time I've ever spent with her.' Laurel didn't add *thankfully* but Eloise could hear it in her voice.

'She was…' Cruel. Evil. Nightmarish. A total witch in a blonde wig. 'She liked to be the centre of attention,' Eloise said, conscious that Laurel *was* Melissa's sister, despite everything. She'd only met Laurel at the start of the wedding planning, six months ago, and most of their conversations so far had been wedding-related—with the occasional frustrated eye-roll and knowing glance when Melissa video-called in from LA with another hundred demands. But since Laurel had arrived at Morwen Hall the day before to set up for the wedding, Eloise had found it hard to believe that she and Melissa had even *one* parent in common, they were so different.

They had the same ambition, though. While Melissa had channelled hers into stardom, Laurel had taken a quieter route—setting up her own wedding planning company that was just starting to be featured in bridal magazines and websites. Of the two paths, Eloise felt strangely more envious of Laurel's than Melissa's. Eloise had never wanted to be a star, not really. But her own business… She shook her head. She had a good job at Morwen Hall. One she didn't plan to jeopardise by daydreaming.

'The centre of attention. I can believe that,' Laurel said with feeling. 'I guess maybe she feels she missed out on that, growing up. I mean, with our father staying with my mum instead of hers for so long.'

'Perhaps,' Eloise allowed. 'But I reckon she made up for it by stealing all my boyfriends.' She slapped her hand across her mouth as the words came out, but Laurel just laughed.

'*All* of them? How many did you have?'

'Two,' Eloise said mournfully. 'At different times, obviously. And, on both occasions, your sister managed to convince them that they'd be better off with someone else. Usually her.'

It hadn't been too hard either. Growing up in the same town, going to the same school *and* working at the same hotel meant that Melissa had known all of Eloise's secrets. She'd known every embarrassing story to tell about her family, and which ones to pick for maximum effect.

And she'd had more than enough to choose from.

'Well, at least you won't have to worry about her doing that this time,' Laurel said.

'Well, no,' Eloise agreed. 'Since I don't have a boyfriend.' And hadn't had one for quite a while, actually, not that she was counting days. She'd rather wait and find the *right* one than try out any guy who came calling.

Not that she'd had any significant success since leaving school. In fact, the boyfriends Melissa had lured away might be considered the highlights of her dating career. Certainly a lot better than the one who'd left her for her mother. Or the guy at university who'd managed to screw her over both personally *and* professionally.

Maybe she just wasn't born to date. Heaven knew her mother had done enough dating for the both of them.

Laurel rolled her eyes. 'I meant I really think she's properly in love with Riley.'

Eloise found it hard to imagine Melissa loving *anybody* besides herself, but then maybe she'd changed. Organising weddings didn't tend to bring out the best in people. Maybe most of the time she was a total sweetheart.

Actually, no. That was even harder to imagine.

Still... 'I hope so,' Eloise said. 'I hope she's truly happy.'

Because the happier Melissa was, the better the chances of the wedding going off without a hitch, Melissa and Riley riding off into the sunset together and Eloise never having to see either of them again.

'Me too,' Laurel said. 'If only so I never have to organise another wedding for her. I mean, I know this is a huge coup for my new business and everything, but still...'

Eloise laughed, ignoring the pang of envy she felt at the excitement in Laurel's voice when she talked about her company. 'At least being the wedding planner means you got out of having to be maid of honour. I mean, have you seen those dresses she picked?'

Laurel pulled a face, probably feeling slightly queasy at the memory of the miles of icy blue-green satin and chiffon that had been sacrificed to make the bridesmaids and maid of honour dresses. 'Actually, it was never even suggested. I think Melissa was pretty set on having Cassidy Haven as maid of honour from the start. The celeb factor, you know.'

'You're probably right,' Eloise agreed. As far as she knew, Melissa and Cassidy's acquaintance went back to approximately one film, in which they had two scenes together. But, given Cassidy's rising star and box office gold reputation, that would be enough for Melissa.

A crunching noise echoed from the end of the driveway, getting closer. The sound of tyres on frozen ground, Eloise knew from experience. 'They're here,' she said, and Laurel raised her eyebrows with surprise.

'They are? Where?'

'Just coming around the bend.' At her words, the large black four-by-four appeared from the tree cover and Eloise pasted on her smile. Time to start the show.

Laurel straightened her skirt and her shoulders,

trying to pull herself up to her full height, Eloise supposed, although Eloise still had a full head and shoulders on her. She usually did with most people.

The four-by-four slowed to a halt in front of Morwen Hall and the driver stepped out to open the rear door. Eloise was vaguely aware of the passenger door opening too, but her gaze was firmly fixed on the blonde stepping out of the back seat, knees together, a picture of English elegance. Her light hair was fixed perfectly back from her beautiful face, her pale pink lipstick unsmudged. She hadn't even spilt any coffee on her snowy white jumper—cashmere, Eloise was sure—and white trousers.

Maybe celebrities really were another species. No human should look that good after an eleven-hour flight.

Eloise recognised Riley Black from the engagement photos and the occasional video call he joined them for during the wedding planning. He smiled up at them as he came around from the other side of the car to take his fiancée's arm. Laurel moved down a few steps to greet them and

Eloise finally turned her attention to the fourth occupant of the car.

And promptly lost the ability to breathe.

Noah Cross had learned fairly early in his career how to tune out the meaningless chatter that came with the job but still pay just enough attention to assure whoever was talking that he was listening to them. The skill had served him well on movie sets across the world, in press junkets and at awards ceremonies.

Until he'd met Melissa Sommers.

The whole flight from LA he'd been trying to read a new script his agent, Tessa, had sent him, to 'keep you too busy at this damn wedding to get into any trouble', as she'd put it. Normally, he'd have tossed the script in his suitcase, relaxed with a drink on the flight and looked forward to seducing a bridesmaid or two, just to keep in practice. But this script was from a writer he admired, one he'd dreamt of working with for too long now—Queenie Walters. Her films were renowned for being deep, thought-provoking, meaningful—and for winning every award going. Basically, the opposite of the sort of films he'd been making for the last seven years.

The sort of films that had led to Riley Black asking him to be his best man somewhere in the middle of nowhere, England, in minus temperatures in December.

Maybe it was time to start making a new sort of film.

So, back to the script.

It was good, that much he could tell, even from one cursory reading with Melissa chattering in his ear and Riley chiming in every few minutes or so. He could even tell it through the champagne he'd drunk to make the journey just a little more bearable.

He wanted to make this film. More than that, he wanted to *star* in this film.

He knew that the leading role wasn't the one his agent had suggested him for—that would be the light relief, the comic best friend. It was his own fault. He'd told Tessa he wanted to do something different, something other than action blockbusters and superhero movies. And she'd taken the not absurd mental leap and assumed he wanted comedy. She'd sent him a raft of terrible slapstick-without-humour typescripts to start with, until he'd asked for something a little...*better*.

Then she'd sent him *Eight Days After* and he'd known she understood at last.

Well, almost. She still saw him as the supporting actor.

He needed to convince her—and the director—that he was Best Actor material.

'And then she suggested that maybe I didn't need to have a veil at all!' Melissa crowed with laughter, regaling them all with yet another tale about her wedding planner, apparently oblivious to the fact that her fiancé had already heard it, the driver of the car didn't care and Noah was working very hard on not listening. 'Not have a veil! Can you imagine?'

'I heard that Rochelle Twist didn't have a veil at her wedding,' Noah said from the front seat, not looking up from his script.

'She didn't?' Melissa's eyes widened with alarm and Noah knew for certain that she would walk down the aisle without the veil on New Year's Eve. Well, unless she checked the Internet for photographic proof and realised that Noah was making it up to mess with her. As if he had any idea at all what A-list actresses wore on their wedding days.

It was still weird to think that he was up there on their invitation lists. The fact that Riley had asked him to be best man after just three films said a lot. Noah liked the guy well enough, but he wouldn't call him a best friend. They'd been out and got drunk a few times, played some poker. And Noah had spent one very long night listening to Riley weigh up the pros and cons of asking Melissa to marry him—the main pros apparently being 'it'd be great for my image' and 'she really wants to'. But that was about it. Did that qualify him for best man status? Apparently, in Melissa and Riley's eyes, it did.

Seven years ago, it wouldn't have done. Granted, seven years ago Melissa and Riley had probably been teenagers, but still. Back then, Noah had been a nobody, desperate for his big break but secretly afraid it was never going to come—the same as everyone else in town. He'd been living with his best friend Sally, sharing stories of awful auditions, commiserating over rejections with a bottle of cheap wine and trying to pretend that he wasn't crazy about her. Seven years ago, he'd been looking at a future of giving up, going home and admitting to his family that he'd failed, just like they'd said he would.

Then that fabled big break had come—the same day that everything else had been taken away from him.

Noah shook his head, trying to send the memories scattering. He didn't need them today—or any day, for that matter. Life was about the here and now, not the past.

And right now he was about to spend five days in some fancy hotel with a selection of the most beautiful women in the world. Surely he'd be able to find *some* way to pass the time.

The car turned off the main road onto a long sweeping driveway and past a pale sage-green sign with grey lettering, proclaiming the entrance to Morwen Hall. They were there.

Shoving the script back in his hand luggage, Noah peered out of the front windscreen, looking for the Hall itself. He hoped it was as nice as Melissa insisted it would be. He needed a break, a chance to unwind—preferably with company. It had been a long eighteen months making back to back films, plus the promotional efforts. Five days in the middle of nowhere didn't sound all that bad, really. Even if he did have to spend them with Melissa.

The car broke through the last of the trees surrounding the hotel and Morwen Hall loomed into view—all grey stone and huge windows, reflecting the weak winter sun. It looked like something out of a bad Gothic movie, with its turrets and arched windows, and Noah couldn't help but smile at the sight of it. Ostentatious, over the top and not quite the romantic vibe she thought she was going for. It suited Melissa perfectly.

'Isn't it gorgeous? It's *just* as I remember it,' Melissa squealed, and Noah recalled that Morwen Hall wasn't just a venue for her. She'd lived there, or worked there, or something of the sort when she was younger.

Noah looked at the building again and wondered what spending significant time in such a dramatic place would do to a person. Then he looked at Melissa again. *Question answered.*

'Look, honey, Laurel's come out to meet us,' Riley said and Melissa's face soured.

Noah looked to where Riley was pointing and saw two women standing on the steps outside the huge Gothic front door, a wooden creation with twisty ironworks over the top. He couldn't make out their features through the tinted glass, but presumably one of them was the hyper-efficient wedding planner, Laurel, who'd been sending Noah updates and asking him questions for the last six months.

He made a mental note to stay out of her way as much as possible for the next five days. Efficiency grew tiring quickly, he'd found.

The driver opened Melissa's door and the bride swept out. Noah opened his own door and followed, wishing he'd brought his sunglasses as he lost the protection of tinted glass and squinted into the winter sun, looking up at the Hall.

Yep, still just as Gothic.

But the women standing on the steps... The tinted glass definitely hadn't done them justice.

One was a petite brunette, all curves and smiles and bounce as she came down the steps to welcome Melissa with a hug. He hoped that was Laurel, who he'd vowed to avoid. Because the other...

The other stayed standing on the steps, her smile fixed and her hands clasped in front of her. She looked uncomfortable, as if she'd rather be anywhere else in the world. As if she was trying to fade into the background—something Noah wasn't used to seeing in the circles he hung out in these days.

She'd never manage it, though. She had to be nearly six foot in her sensible black heels, almost as tall as he was, and her pale features were topped with a cloud of blazing red hair, pinned tightly back to reveal the classical beauty of her features. He couldn't see the colour of her eyes from this distance, but he wanted to. He wanted to know if they were as striking as the rest of her.

Then she turned to look at him and he knew it didn't matter what colour they were—if this woman was looking at him, he'd never see anything else.

This woman would never disappear into the background *anywhere*.

And Noah hoped to be seeing an awful lot more of her over the next five days. Maybe he'd even get to find out what that beautiful hair looked like tumbling around her naked shoulders...

Shouldering his bag, he put on his most charming smile, hoped that the effect of the champagne had mostly passed and strode towards the imposing front door of Morwen Hall, and the equally imposing woman standing in front of it.

Maybe this wedding wouldn't be a complete disaster after all.

Noah Cross. Noah freaking Cross.

Okay, breathing was becoming an issue now. She really had to get hold of herself.

Eloise broke away from staring at the ridiculously handsome Noah Cross and sucked in a good lungful of crisp December air to replace all the oxygen that had been knocked out of her at the sight of him.

She was being ridiculous. *Of course* he was good-looking. He was a movie star. It was part of the deal. It definitely didn't mean anything important—that he was a nice person, or someone she wanted to spend time with. In fact, in her experience, it meant the exact opposite.

No. She was not her mother. She would not let her head be turned by the first attractive—*gorgeous*—man who looked her way. Hadn't she just decided that dating wasn't for her?

He probably wasn't even looking at her. He was probably looking at Morwen Hall. It was, after all, even more striking than her red hair, and considerably more beautiful.

That thought sobered her right up and knocked her back into business mode. She had a wedding to host, and an arch nemesis to deal with while she was doing it. She did *not* have time to get sidetracked ogling movie stars—especially given how many of them would be arriving later that afternoon.

Making sure her best fake smile was still in place, Eloise descended the front steps to join Melissa, Laurel and Riley on the driveway.

'Eloise!' Melissa cried, with what had to be phoney enthusiasm. 'It's just so *wonderful* to see you again, honey.' The 'honey' was new, Eloise noted, as Melissa leant forward to kiss the air a few inches away from Eloise's icy cheeks. Presumably something else she'd picked up in Hollywood, along with the fiancé.

'You've seen me on video calls for the last six months, Melissa,' Eloise said, still smiling so hard her cheeks ached.

'Oh, but that's not the same thing *at all*.' Melissa stretched a slender white arm around Laurel and Eloise's shoulders. 'Isn't this just *perfect?*

My *oldest* friend and my favourite *half*-sister, working together to give me the wedding of my dreams.'

'It sure is perfect, honey,' Riley agreed, his southern accent far more pronounced than in his films.

Of course she'd think it's perfect, Eloise thought. *She's got the two people she wants to make miserable most in the world waiting on her hand and foot as the culmination of six months of demanding the impossible from them. It's her every dream come true.*

Apparently Hollywood stardom wasn't enough for some people. They had to come back and crush the little people they left behind too.

She glanced to her left and caught Laurel's eye, wondering if the wedding planner was having the exact same thoughts. Even if she was, neither of them would say anything, not with their careers riding on this. That was probably what Melissa was banking on. That, or she honestly thought they were grateful to her for condescending to use their services for her wedding.

Actually, knowing Melissa, it was probably the latter.

Eloise bit her tongue all the same, reminding herself of what really mattered: her promotion. If she pulled off this wedding, Mr Richards, who owned Morwen Hall, had promised her that she'd be made permanent manager in the New Year. Not to mention the huge boost the hotel would get from the exposure. That was a good thing. A good, secure job with a hotel that was doing well. That was a sensible career goal.

All she had to do was make it through to January the first without telling Melissa what she really thought of her, or giving her any reason to complain about Eloise's professionalism. How hard could that be?

Oh, yeah. Very.

But Eloise was determined to do it all the same.

'This is quite some place, Melissa. I can absolutely see why you chose it. It's perfect for you!' Noah Cross's voice was weirdly familiar from those times she'd sat in cinemas watching him beat up bad guys and seduce beautiful women on screen. It was just plain odd to hear him apply those dulcet tones to Morwen Hall. 'Moody, well built…and I guess it has one hell of a history.'

His upbeat tone made the comment sound complimentary but, as he met her eyes, Eloise realised he knew *exactly* what he was saying. The humour in his gaze only grew as Melissa frowned—not enough to cause lines, though—and said, 'Well, yes. It is quite special.'

It was a shame Noah Cross was an actor, Eloise thought. Otherwise, she had a feeling he might be exactly her sort of person.

'Why don't you all step inside?' she said, deflecting Noah's observations. 'It's freezing out here and I'd love to show you all around the old place, tell you a bit about its history.'

Noah sprung up the steps beside her, even as Melissa said, 'Of course, I already know everything there is to know about Morwen Hall.'

Eloise's smile became a little more fixed. 'I think you'll find we've changed a *few* things since you were last here, Melissa.' *Eight years ago*.

'Well, I for one can't wait to learn all about this place.' Noah slapped his hand against the heavy wood of the front door and the ironwork rang out an echo. 'And whether or not there are any vampires hiding in there waiting to suck my blood.' He flashed a smile that Eloise couldn't help but return.

'No vampires,' she promised. At least, as long as you didn't count Melissa. 'But I can't promise you might not see the odd ghost.'

Noah raised his eyebrows. 'I don't believe in ghosts.'

'That's good.' Eloise grinned back at him. 'Better just hope they don't believe in film stars either.'

Noah laughed, warm and dark and deep, and Eloise tore her gaze away from him. She didn't need to notice the way he tipped his head back when he laughed, or the long line of his neck, or his designer stubble. It was all totally irrelevant to her, and her job.

But she stole another look before heading back inside all the same.

CHAPTER TWO

THE INSIDE OF Morwen Hall was rather more what Noah had been expecting than the weirdly Gothic exterior. With its calming pale green walls and dove-grey trim, the luxurious but comfortable velvet and leather sofas in the main lobby and the deep pile rugs laid over the original stone floor, it was hard to believe Eloise's stories of ghosts. Inside, Morwen Hall could be any luxury five-star hotel anywhere in the world. Still, Noah couldn't shake the feeling that there might be more to this house, under the surface, than its owners wanted anyone to see.

And more to its manager too. Noah found his gaze fixed on Eloise as she shrugged off her pale grey coat, revealing a demure charcoal skirt suit beneath that went perfectly with the sensible black heels. He supposed that with such arresting hair and eyes brightly coloured clothing was just overkill.

Still, he couldn't help but imagine what she'd look like in the sort of dresses the actresses he knew wore on the red carpet. Something that showed off her figure instead of hiding it. Noah was a connoisseur of women's figures, and Eloise's definitely looked like one he'd like to explore further.

'Melissa, Riley, would you like me to show you to your suite?' Eloise asked. Noah supposed it was only polite to deal with the bride and groom first. Besides, it would mean she had more time for him afterwards—and more time for him to talk her into having a drink together later.

Melissa frowned ever so slightly, a tiny line appearing between her eyebrows. 'Actually, I need to speak with my wedding planner.' She slipped a hand through the crook of Laurel's arm and led her off to the side. 'Why don't you get our best man settled first?'

Noah hefted his carry-on bag over his shoulder. He hadn't seen his suitcase since the airport so he assumed it was being dealt with somewhere, and would magically appear in his room when he needed it. He loved hotels. They were almost as good as film sets for having your every need seen to before you even knew what you needed.

'You'll turn into one of those puffed up idiots who don't know the value of a hard day's work.'

His dad's voice in his head made Noah scowl, as it always did, but he shook the expression away before Eloise turned to face him and replaced it with his habitual charming smile.

'Right. Okay.' Eloise surveyed him with something akin to displeasure on her face, which gave Noah slight pause. Usually, women were *delighted* to score some alone time with him. And, from the way Eloise had stared at him on arrival, he'd naively assumed that she'd be the same.

Apparently, he was missing something here.

'If you'll just follow me, Mr Cross?' Eloise said, every inch the professional, as she headed for the elevators at the back of the lobby. They had a Gothic-style metalwork design painted on the doors, which amused Noah. As an attempt to make them fit in with the rest of the surroundings of Morwen Hall, he supposed it was as good a try as any.

'Guess these didn't come with the building, huh?' he asked as she pressed the button to call one. 'The elevators, I mean. Sorry. They're "lifts" here, right?'

'That's right,' Eloise said with a nod. 'And no. They didn't have lifts when Morwen Hall was built.'

From her tone, Noah suspected she was already writing him off as a dumb American movie star. Well, she wouldn't be the first—hadn't his own father done the same? And there had been plenty more since—journalists, interviewers, all sorts. It was always fun to prove them wrong.

'Gothic revival, right? So, nineteenth-century? I'd guess…1850?'

If she was surprised Eloise didn't show it. '1848, actually. At least that was when work started.'

'Sounds like you know a lot about the place. Have you worked here long?'

The elevator pinged and the doors opened. Eloise motioned for him to enter first, which he did, then she stepped in behind him, pressing the button for the top floor.

'Since I was sixteen,' she said as the doors swished shut.

Of course. She was Melissa's oldest friend. She, and the Hall, were presumably the reason they were having the wedding in England in December in the first place. 'And that's when you met Melissa, right. Nice of her to want to come back here for the wedding, I guess.'

'It's just lovely,' Eloise said, her tone flat.

Noah was beginning to suspect that 'oldest friends' might not be the most accurate of descriptions for Eloise and Melissa's relationship.

'She must have a lot of fond memories of working here,' he pressed.

'I'm sure she does.' Eloise didn't place any extra emphasis on the word 'she', but somehow Noah heard it. From what he knew about Melissa, he wasn't overly surprised. Oh, she was sweetness and light to directors, producers and other stars, but he'd seen her berate one of the catering assistants for not having *exactly* the right kind of chia seed for her salad. He knew that sort of person—who could be anything you wanted if you mattered, and hell on wheels if you didn't. Hollywood was full of them.

He prided himself on trying not to ever become one of them. Whatever his father thought.

He'd learned how to be a star and still be gracious from watching Sally. It was one of the many lessons his best friend had taught him. After she got a recurring role in a weekly drama, she'd still been, well, Sally. Lovely and sweet and kind and patient with everyone from her co-stars to the guy on the street begging for enough quarters to buy a coffee. Sally had been the most genuine person he'd known in a city full of actors.

Just remembering that much pricked at his heart and Noah knew it was time to change the subject.

'Enough about Melissa,' he said as the elevator reached its destination and the doors parted again. 'So you've worked here, what, eight years?' He'd guess ten, based on Melissa's age, but everyone liked a little flattery, right?

'Ten, actually,' Eloise corrected him, and he hid a smile. He still had it.

'Must have seen a lot of changes here.' That was a given too, right? Everything changed. Whether you wanted it to or not.

'Yep. Melissa left, for one.' Eloise shut her eyes briefly. 'Sorry. I shouldn't have said that.'

'Yes, you should,' Noah insisted. Not least because it was the first real thing she'd said since they'd met and for some reason—perhaps because he'd been remembering Sally—Noah wanted her to be real. Maybe it was just that he had enough fakes in his professional life already—not that it usually bothered him. People who were putting on an act, being who they thought you wanted them to be, never wanted you to look too deep or get too close, so they never looked too deep or too close in return. And that suited Noah perfectly.

Too deep and too close led to the sort of pain he wasn't willing to feel again.

But Eloise... Maybe it would do him good to see some reality again. As long as *he* wasn't the one getting real.

'So... Oldest friend?' he asked as she led him along a wide corridor, carpeted in deep, dark green pile. They really did go all out with the luxury at this place. Not that Noah was complaining. He'd worked hard for years to earn this sort of luxury. He deserved it. And he would ignore any and all voices inside his head that said otherwise. Even if they did sound like Dad.

What was it about this place that was dredging up all those old insecurities he thought he'd left behind seven years ago? He bit back a laugh. Hadn't Eloise warned him he might find ghosts here?

'We've known each other pretty much all our lives.' Eloise sighed. 'Born in the same hospital, went to the same playgroup, same schools, then had the same part-time jobs as chambermaids here at Morwen Hall.'

'So you basically lived the same lives until Melissa set out to conquer Hollywood?' Interesting. He'd expect Eloise to show a little more envy, in that case, but mostly she just seemed…inconvenienced by Melissa's arrival.

'Not *exactly* the same lives,' Eloise said. 'But yes, there were similarities, I suppose.'

'And you never fancied Hollywood?' With Eloise's striking looks, he was pretty sure she'd have found some work at least. But Eloise laughed.

'No, not for me.'

'How come?'

She paused outside door number three-one-nine and flashed him a smile. 'Too many actors. Now, let me show you your room.'

He was *almost* sure she was joking, Noah decided, as Eloise gave him the nickel and dime tour of his suite. For all that Morwen Hall was unlike any building he'd ever been in from the outside, he'd expected the rooms to be fairly standard. 'Luxury hotel' didn't have so many different meanings, in his experience.

The main room of the suite confirmed his guess—there were a couple of creamy sofas, a coffee table laden with magazines and local information, a large window with a round table and two wooden chairs in front of it, a TV, fridge, desk, the usual. But then Eloise led him through to the bedroom.

'Huh.' Noah stared at the giant four-poster bed in the middle of the bedroom, decked out with heavy forest-green drapes and blankets over crisp white sheets. The wall behind the bed had been left bare, exposing the original stone of the house, but with tapestries hung either side of the four-poster for warmth. A pile of cushions and pillows in varying shades of green and different textures sat by the wooden headboard, ready to sink into.

'Do you like it?' Eloise asked and, for the first time, Noah heard a hint of uncertainty in her voice. 'With Melissa and Riley out in the Gatehouse suite, this is the best room in the hotel.'

'It looks it,' Noah said, eyeing the bed apprecia-
tively. He had some awesome ideas for that bed.

He turned his attention back to Eloise, wondering if she might be willing to help him out with
some of them. Given the way she was backing
away, probably not.

'Well, if you're all settled...'

'What are you doing this evening?' Sometimes you just had to take your chances, Noah
had learnt. And right then he needed a distraction from all the thoughts of the past that had
been plaguing him since he'd arrived—since he'd
started reading that script, he realised. *That* was
it. It wasn't about ghosts, just a story that hit too
close to home.

Still, a night with Eloise would probably cure
that too.

'Melissa and Riley have planned a welcome
drinks party in the Saloon for all their guests,'
Eloise said promptly. 'If you head down to reception for seven—'

'You'll be there?' Noah gave her his warmest smile, feeling she might be missing the point
slightly.

'In my capacity as Hotel Manager? Absolutely.'

Definitely missing the point. Was she just shy, star-struck or honestly indifferent to him? Noah couldn't tell. A perverse part of him almost hoped it was the last option. It had been too long since a woman had offered him a real challenge.

'In that case, I'm looking forward to it,' Noah said. Perhaps he'd fit a nap in before seven. That would get him back on his game.

But first he had to finish reading the script before his agent called to ask what he thought.

Work before fun, whatever the press wrote about him.

'Great,' Eloise said, sounding as if she was dreading every second. 'I'll see you then.'

As the door shut behind her, Noah made himself a promise. Before Melissa and Riley said 'I do' he'd get Eloise the Hotel Manager to warm up to him—or even warm him up.

No one ever said that Noah Cross wasn't up for a challenge.

Eloise shut Noah's door behind her and felt every muscle in her body relax for the first time since she'd spotted him outside the hotel. The last thing she needed this week was a distraction—let alone a stupid girlish crush.

Sucking in a deep breath, Eloise made a resolution before striding down the corridor back towards the lifts: under no circumstances would she allow a ridiculous attraction—to a *film star* of all people—to derail any of the plans for Melissa and Riley's wedding.

All she needed to do, she reminded herself as she waited for the lift, was to make it to January the first. Then her lovely, normal, sensible and stable life would return and she could forget all about Melissa Sommers until her inevitable divorce and remarriage. No, even then, surely Melissa wouldn't return to the scene of the crime, so to speak. It had to be bad form to hold a second wedding at the same venue as the first.

If this wedding went well, it could be the last time she had to see Melissa Sommers—ever. If that wasn't motivation to not mess it up, nothing was.

Downstairs in the lobby, Melissa was still berating Laurel about something or other. Eloise got close enough to hear the words 'wedding favours' and 'an embarrassment' and backed off to loiter at the reception desk until they were finished. Anything wedding-related that wasn't actually part of the venue was, unfortunately for Laurel, Laurel's problem. And, as much as she liked Melissa's half-sister, Eloise had enough problems of her own at Morwen Hall without borrowing other people's.

After a few minutes where Eloise pretended to check the reservations system on the computer, Laurel approached, her smile fixed and tight. 'I'm afraid I'm going to have to abandon you for a few hours. Melissa needs me to pop up to London.'

'Wedding favours?'

Laurel nodded. 'Apparently the ones we decided on three months ago are now passé and embarrassing.'

'Of course.' Eloise sighed. There was no way to tell whether Melissa was seriously unhappy with the favours or just trying to make Laurel's life difficult. Either way, Laurel would need to fix it. 'So, what's the plan?'

'Apparently she's made some calls and there are now one hundred and fifty alternative favours—something to do with artisan chocolates and mini personalised perfumes, I think—waiting at some boutique in central London. So I'm off to pick them up.'

'A wedding planner's work is never done.'

'Especially not with this wedding.' Laurel gave her a tired smile. 'Anyway, I'm going to hitch a lift with the next car arriving from the airport and get it to drop me off on its way to pick up the next set of guests—there should just about be time, as long as the traffic's not too awful.'

'How will you get back?' Eloise asked because she probably shouldn't grab hold of Laurel's leg and beg her not to leave her alone with these awful people.

'The last car heading back from the airport will have to swing past and pick me up.' Laurel sighed. 'And I'll just have to pray that the guest inside isn't some absurdly high maintenance celeb that objects to travelling with the help—or taking a significant detour.'

Eloise laughed. 'I cannot *imagine* where you might have got the idea that Melissa would be friends with that sort of person.'

'I know, right?' Laurel smiled again, a real grin this time. Then her expression turned more serious. 'Will you be okay here without me? Really? I know there's still masses to do…'

Eloise waved away her concerns with a flap of her hand. Laurel panicking all over London wouldn't help either of them, or get this wedding going. 'I'll be fine. Everything's set up for the welcome drinks, and Chef's already in the kitchen working on the canapés and such, so I'm free to supervise the check-ins. Once I've shown Melissa and Riley to the Bridal Suite, anyway. I hope they like it.'

'How could they not? It's gorgeous.' Laurel tugged the strap of her messenger bag higher up on her shoulder. 'Right, I'd better go. Good luck!'

'You too. May all your favours be cutting edge and perfect.'

'That's the hope!' Laurel waved as she shoved the heavy front door open with her shoulder, and then Eloise was alone with Melissa and Riley. Exactly the scenario she'd been hoping to avoid.

With a bright smile, Eloise turned to walk towards the bride and groom, who were indulging in a nauseating public display of affection in her lobby. Because this week wasn't awkward enough already.

'If you two are ready, I'd love to show you both to our Bridal Suite. I think you'll agree it's something a bit special.'

Melissa pulled away from Riley, who kept his hand low on her hip. 'I can't wait to see it! You've converted the old gatehouse, Laurel said?'

She sounded enthusiastic enough, which gave Eloise hope. Maybe Melissa *had* grown up at last and all the tensions of the last six months were just the usual stresses of being a bride, plus the added stress of doing it all in the limelight. It seemed unlikely but Eloise lived in hope.

'That's right,' she said, leading them out of the hotel's front door and down the steps to the driveway. 'It's just a short walk from the Hall proper, but we find that our happy couples enjoy the privacy.'

Riley's mouth twitched into a grin at that. 'I bet they do. I know I plan to!'

Melissa dodged his hands as he grabbed for her waist again. For a moment she looked so girlish and young that they could all have been sixteen again. Except, Eloise reminded herself, if they were, she definitely wouldn't have been invited to hang out with them.

'Not until after the wedding, you don't!' Melissa squealed as she danced across the driveway in her ridiculously expensive leather boots and impractical bright white coat. Her blonde hair shone in the winter sunlight, her pale skin flawless as she smiled.

It was, Eloise decided, a good job she wasn't the jealous type.

'Can you believe it?' Riley asked, falling into step with Eloise. 'She's making me wait until after the wedding. I have the most beautiful fiancée in the world and I'm not even allowed to touch her.'

'Oh, like you haven't touched me plenty before,' Melissa said with a flirtatious laugh. 'I seem to remember you could barely do anything else for the first month or two...'

Eloise picked up the pace just a bit, relieved when the Gatehouse came into view around the edge of the trees.

'Not for the last forty-eight hours!' Riley protested. 'It's cruel and unusual torture; that's what it is. Eloise agrees, don't you?'

Eloise pretty much thought it was none of her

business, and she'd rather keep it that way, but the client was the client.

'I think that seeing the Bridal Suite might tempt her resolve,' she said diplomatically.

'That's why he won't be staying in it until the wedding night.' Melissa's tone was triumphant, and the small smile on her face as she looked at Eloise made it clear that she knew exactly what she was doing. 'Oh, didn't Laurel tell you that Riley would need a separate room until Saturday?'

Eloise bit the inside of her cheek in a desperate attempt to keep a hold on her temper. Melissa knew perfectly well that she hadn't—probably because she'd never mentioned it to Laurel in the first place. In fact, Eloise suspected that she'd just come up with it at that moment and was now using the idea to play Eloise and Laurel off each other. That would be just the sort of thing she would do.

Well. Eloise might have fallen for it when she was sixteen. But she wasn't sixteen any longer.

'Actually, she did suggest it might be a possibility so I've got a very special room put aside for Riley in the hotel, just in case he needed it.'

Riley looked impressed. Melissa looked murderous. Eloise smiled serenely and moved past them both to unlock the door to the Gatehouse.

'Now, how about we take a look at where you'll be spending your first night as man and wife?' she said. Then she could get onto building an extra hotel suite for Riley. There had to be a solution somewhere. She just hadn't thought of it yet.

Even Melissa had to be impressed by the Gatehouse Suite, and Riley's eyes were huge as Eloise gave them the tour. Morwen Hall was a luxury hotel from top to bottom but the Gatehouse kicked that luxury up a notch further. The stone building had been completely renovated— walls had been knocked through to turn what had been a small family home into a spacious suite for two. Downstairs was laid out as an open-plan living area, with a small kitchen counter running along one side. It wasn't a functioning kitchen—that wasn't what guests needed here. Instead, it had a small fridge filled with champagne and another stuffed with high-end chocolates, caviar and other delicious treats. A top of the range coffee machine with quality china fulfilled guests' caffeine needs, and an extensive menu was available twenty-four hours from direct dial to the front desk.

Downstairs was, Eloise thought proudly, impressive. But upstairs blew it away.

The four-poster bed that dominated the room was larger even than the one that had rendered Noah speechless. The bed linens were snowy white Egyptian cotton, with luxurious touches in jewel-coloured satin and silk accessories. The large bay window—complete with cushioned window seat—looked out over the river, and the en suite bathroom featured both an ultra-modern shower for two and an old-fashioned roll top bath.

'It's gorgeous,' Melissa admitted eventually. Then, apparently unable to resist criticising *something,* she added, 'And I'm sure I'll be fine, all the way out here.'

It's two minutes from the hotel. Less if you don't stop to grope your fiancé.

'Well, I'll make sure you have my room number,' Riley said, wrapping an arm around Melissa's waist and giving the four-poster a good, long look. 'Just in case you need me to come down here and…save you.'

Rolling her eyes, Melissa pushed him away.

'You and Eloise should go and find your room. I'm going to take advantage of that lovely bath.'

'Right,' Eloise said, thinking fast. 'Your room. Just follow me!'

As they left Melissa to her bath, Eloise spotted the first of the guests' cars pulling up the driveway. She was out of time, and all chaos was likely to break loose soon. And Riley still needed a room, even if she doubted he'd actually end up sleeping in it at all.

Mentally, she ran through the rooming list for the wedding in her head. After Noah's, the next best room in the hotel had been earmarked for Riley's brother, Dan. He wasn't bringing a guest, so at least that would only be one person to re-house. Plus his flight was the last one in, so that gave her more time to try and fix things. And if the worst came to the worst and she couldn't magic another room from a no-show, or persuade Melissa to let Riley back into the Gatehouse, at least Dan and Riley might not be *too* horrified about having to share…

It was the best she could do for now. Decision made, Eloise covered the distance between the Gatehouse and Morwen Hall with large strides, leaving Riley trying to keep up. She'd show him to his room then get back down to supervise check-in. Laurel would be back to help—and provide much-needed moral support—before the welcome drinks.

And then all Eloise had to do was resist the considerable charms of Noah Cross for the evening.

How hard could that be?

Then she remembered Noah's smile, and realised that there was a very real possibility that she might be doomed.

CHAPTER THREE

IN THE END, the nap had to wait.

Noah placed the script reverently on the bed in front of him and reached for his phone without ever looking away from the cover sheet. He didn't want to break the magic spell the writing had cast over him before he spoke to his agent. He wanted to live in this feeling—in the brilliance and excitement of a perfect story. The way he felt he knew every one of the characters inside out as if he *was* the characters.

This film—this was the one he'd been waiting for.

He couldn't remember being this excited about a part since... Well, since he'd first moved to LA with Sally.

Swallowing hard at the memory, he pushed it aside and punched the right combination on the screen to call Tessa, his agent.

'I want this part,' he said, the moment she picked up.

'Noah?' She sounded sleepy. Noah did a quick mental calculation of the time difference and winced. Then he decided that, since she was awake now anyway, he might as well continue.

'*Eight Days After*,' he said. 'I want the part. The lead. None of this supporting actor stuff. I want the main attraction.'

'Really?' Tessa was awake now, if the pep in her voice was anything to go by. 'You think you're right for Marcus?'

'Definitely,' Noah replied, ignoring the surprise in her voice. 'Trust me. They want me in that role. I will knock it out of the park.' There was a pause on the other line, and Noah's confidence took a slight dip. But not for long. He hadn't got where he was by letting criticism knock him back. 'What? What did they say about me? You might as well just tell me—you know I'll hear it eventually anyway.' That was how Hollywood gossip worked. Confidences were never kept, and secrets always got out. You just had to front it out and live with whatever people had to say about you, Noah had found. He just didn't let the gibes and the comments get past his defences any more. They didn't hurt if he didn't let himself feel them.

'Stefan, the director…he's worried you might not have the, well, depth for the part.'

'For Marcus?'

'For the best friend part.'

Noah blinked. 'The best friend *has* no depth. He's basically there to lighten the mood so that no one slits their wrists in the movie theatres.' If Stefan didn't believe he could even pull off *that* part, Noah had a harder path to climb than even he'd anticipated.

'Still. This is a very different movie to the sort you've been in before.'

'Lately,' Noah countered.

'Since you became an actor anyone has heard of,' Tessa shot back, and Noah winced. Had it really been that long since he'd made a film that *mattered?* He knew that it had. He'd not taken on a part with substance since he'd got his big break in a summer blockbuster.

So why now? Why this one?

Noah shook his head. It didn't matter why. It only mattered that he get it. One way or another.

'What will it take to convince him?' he asked.

'That you can play the best friend?'

'No.'

Tessa sighed. 'Look, Noah, I think they've already got someone in the frame for Marcus—and no, before you ask, I don't know who. They're being cagey, though, so that probably means someone big.'

'Someone they're not sure of, or they'd be telling everyone.'

'Maybe. Why does this matter so much to you?' Tessa asked. 'I mean, you've been perfectly happy for years playing the big budget hero, the action guy or whatever.'

'You mean as a more looks than talent kind of actor,' Noah translated. He'd heard the talk as well as she had.

'You said it, not me. But yeah. So what's changed?'

Noah sank back against the pillows on the four-poster bed, trying to find the right words. 'It's… it's this script. I mean, I knew I was ready for a change. It's been seven years since…' Since he'd taken a part that made him look too deep, search too far to find the character. Since he'd done anything more than drift through his roles without having to think too much about the emotions behind them. Since he'd risked feeling at all.

'Since what happened to Sally.' Tessa was one of the few people who knew that story. One of the many reasons Noah had stuck with her as his agent even after he had agencies banging on his door wanting to sign him.

'Yeah. But it's more than that. There's something about this script, Tess.' Something that made his heart race, made him want to reach for something more, something better, something deeper, for the first time in a long time. 'The way it talks about the human condition, about loss, and connection and love...'

'I know,' Tessa said quietly. 'That was why I was surprised you want to do it. They're usually exactly the things you try to avoid.'

That was the problem with having the same agent for almost a decade. They got to know you—and your weaknesses—too well.

'Yeah, well, maybe it's time for a change.' In career terms, if not personally.

'Okay, be honest. Is this about that interview last month?'

'You know I don't let those things get to me.'

Even if they *had* said that his films were getting more brainless by the season.

'That one would get to anyone. There's no shame in wanting to make better movies, Noah.'

'Exactly!' Better movies. That was the goal. And totally achievable without opening himself up to all the things he'd built walls against years before. 'So you'll get me the part?'

'I'll get you a video call with the director,' Tessa corrected. 'That's the most I can do. Then it's up to you. But you're really going to have to blow them away.' The warning was clear in her voice. They didn't want him for the part. If he wanted it…he'd have to show them they couldn't do it right without him.

'I will.'

'I mean it. This part needs real feeling and—'

'You don't think I can do it,' Noah realised. 'And here I thought agents were supposed to be an actor's biggest cheerleader.'

'I can dig out the skirt and pom-poms if you like.' Tessa sighed again. 'Look, I know you *used* to be able to do it. That's why I signed you.'

'And I thought it was for my pretty face.'

'That too,' she admitted. 'But mostly it was

your talent. The way you connected with an audience. But these days… Noah, you don't even connect with the women you sleep with. Be honest. Do you really think you can do this? Look deeper inside yourself and find all that good stuff I haven't seen in years?'

Could he? Noah wasn't sure. 'Honestly, I'm not even sure those parts are still there.'

'Well, if you want this role, you better hope they are.'

'You'll get me the video call?'

'I'll get you the call,' Tessa promised. 'The rest is up to you. But Noah…'

'What?'

'Your acting ability wasn't Stefan's only concern,' Tessa said.

'It should be the only thing that matters,' Noah shot back. 'So what? What else?'

'He doesn't…how did he put it?' Tessa took a breath and started again. 'Stefan wants the film to be the focus, the thing everyone is talking about. Not your love life.'

'I don't have a love life,' Noah pointed out.

He hadn't been in love since Sally died. How could he be?

'You have women. Lots of women, whether you love them or not.'

'I don't.' Why did he have to say it? Tessa already knew. But somehow it felt important to be clear. As if he'd be betraying Sally if he let there be any doubt.

And he already had enough guilt to deal with, knowing he hadn't lived up to being the best friend that she needed.

'You go out with a lot of women and you're seen doing it. People take photos. The photos show up in magazines, on the Internet, and people talk about them.' Tessa's words were clipped, her tone impatient. 'You know this, Noah, and you know the effect it has. Don't be obtuse.'

'The effect it has? The way it drives up ticket sales, you mean?' Because being seen, getting out there, that was as much a part of his job as showing up and playing a part. In some ways it felt like just another part he was playing: Noah Cross, Film Star.

'Not this time,' Tessa said. 'This isn't the sort of film you're used to, Noah. Stefan wants people talking about the meaning, the theme, the soul of the film. Not who you're sleeping with tonight.'

'So you're saying, take the part and give up sex?' Because if that was the case... No, he still wanted the part.

'I'm saying, try a little discretion for once. Okay?'

Discretion. That he could do. 'Fine.'

For a moment, Noah had an image of bright red hair and sparkling eyes. Eloise. With her arresting beauty, she was anything but discreet. Anyone would remember seeing him with her.

Apparently, this wedding had just got a whole lot less fun.

'I'll be discreet,' he promised. 'I'll be so discreet you won't even know I'm here.'

Tessa snorted. 'I'll believe it when I see it.'

By late afternoon, Eloise felt as if her feet might fall off. She'd known the high heels were a mistake. Normally she wore low wedges or boots, but today she'd felt the need for something a little smarter. They weren't even all that high—certainly lower and more sensible than Melissa's expensive spike-heeled boots—but apparently running around Morwen Hall in them all day had beaten her feet into submission. She was ready to retire to the tiny bedrooms they kept for staff members working big events and soak her feet in the not quite full-size bath for an hour or two. Preferably while eating chocolate and sipping red wine.

But, instead, she still had a few more guests to welcome and show to their rooms—including the brother of the groom, who still didn't know his room had been taken over by Riley himself. In all the chaos, Eloise still hadn't found a solution to that either. Unless he wanted her room, and she'd just have to sleep behind the reception desk. She certainly couldn't risk going home, not while Melissa was on the premises. As much as Eloise trusted her deputy manager, she wouldn't leave *anyone* to deal with Melissa alone.

Wearily, Eloise stepped back behind the reception desk and, once she was sure no one could see, slipped her feet from her shoes and let the cool stone floor soothe her feet through her tights. *That* was better.

For a moment, she honestly believed she might get a small break in the craziness of the day to get herself together before the nightmare of the welcome drinks that evening.

Until Melissa's scream cut through the air.

Eloise let her eyes flutter closed just for a moment as she steeled herself for whatever was about to happen. When she opened them again, Melissa was bustling across the lobby, a towel wrapped around her hair, wearing a coat and boots over black silky leggings and a matching top that Melissa obviously classed as loungewear, and probably cost more than Eloise earned in a month.

'Is something the matter, Melissa?' Eloise asked in her calmest, everything-will-be-fine voice. Inside, she just prayed that whatever the problem was, it wasn't the Gatehouse. If Melissa had a problem with the Bridal Suite they really were in trouble.

'It's Cassidy!' Melissa shrieked. 'She just called from Aspen! She's broken her leg on the slopes!'

'Cassidy,' Eloise repeated, her mind running through the guest list again in the hope that this might mean she had a spare room after all... 'Wait, your maid of honour Cassidy?'

'*Yes!*' Eloise winced as the pitch of Melissa's voice reached parts only dogs could hear.

Okay, that was a problem. But Eloise was sure

one of Melissa's other celebrity bridesmaids would be willing to step up to the job. And in the meantime... 'Does that mean she and her family won't be attending the wedding after all?'

And I can give their room to Riley's brother?

Melissa gave her one of those were-you-born-this-stupid looks that Eloise had learned to hate during their childhood. '*Of course* they're coming. Well, not Cassidy—apparently she can't fly. But Dillon—her husband—will still be here. He says he's bringing an "old friend" actually.' The way she said it, Eloise could actually hear the air quotes around the words. She tried not to pull a face, but clearly she was never going to understand celebrity marriages. Who brought their mistress to a friend's wedding when their wife was laid up in hospital?

A melodic chiming noise filled the lobby and Melissa shoved one perfectly manicured hand into her coat pocket and pulled out her phone.

'Kerry? Thank God you called back. Did you hear about Cassidy? Well, what do I do? When are you getting here, anyway? Tomorrow! I need a new maid of honour before tomorrow!'

Kerry, Eloise recalled from many contract negotiations and emails, was Melissa's agent. Why she was the first port of call in a maid of honour crisis, Eloise wasn't sure. But she suspected it was another one of those things she didn't understand about Hollywood.

'Someone who knew me back when? You think we should play up the "local girl made good" angle?' Melissa asked, not bothering to lower her voice at all. 'Isn't it enough that I came back to this dump in the first place?' She rolled her eyes. 'Fine, fine. If that's what you think will sell. Yeah, I'll ask her. Okay. Bye.'

Dump? Had Melissa really just called Morwen Hall a *dump?* It might not have been the peak of luxury ten years ago, but these days it was *spectacular.*

She was so annoyed she was still grinding her teeth in annoyance when Melissa turned back to the reception desk and said, 'Right, change of plan. You're my new maid of honour.'

Eloise blinked. 'What?'

'You.' Melissa pointed at Eloise, jabbing a nail against her breastbone. 'You're going to put on the very expensive pretty dress I've already paid for and walk down the aisle in front of me. You're going to smile for the cameras. You're going to say wonderful things about me, and tell the reporter covering this wedding how close we were growing up, and how Hollywood hasn't changed me at all. *Okay?*'

'Why?' Eloise asked, baffled. Then, as she stared down Melissa's frown, she figured it out. 'This is because of all those articles lately, isn't it? The ones calling you a diva who's forgotten where you came from.'

Melissa sniffed. 'I don't read that sort of trashy magazine.'

'Isn't it the same one that's covering your wedding?' Melissa didn't answer that one. 'So, let me guess. Your agent thinks that if you have an old friend as part of the wedding party it'll show how down-to-earth you still are, with your million-dollar wedding at a five-star hotel.'

'Something like that.'

'Yeah, I'm not doing it.' Not a chance. It was bad enough that she had to put Morwen Hall at the disposal of an ungrateful Melissa and her celebrity mates. The last thing Eloise wanted was to have to be part of this whole debacle. 'Why don't you ask Laurel? She *is* your half-sister.'

Melissa pulled a face. 'No way. Besides, she wouldn't fit in the dress. Have you seen that girl's cleavage?' Eloise had, and was rather envious of it, actually, but she didn't think that would dissuade Melissa.

'The chances are *I* won't fit in the dress either,' Eloise pointed out instead. She knew she was on the skinny side of slender, because that was just how her body and metabolism worked—especially when she was rushing around Morwen Hall all day, every day. But Hollywood celebs were a different category of thin, weren't they? And Eloise *definitely* wasn't that.

'Oh, you will,' Melissa assured her. 'Cassidy had to put weight *on* for her last part, if you can believe it. Something about fat girls being funnier.' Well, that sounded like a film Eloise would go out of her way to avoid. 'So we'll do the dress fitting first thing in the morning then.'

'Wait! I didn't say I'd do it!' But Melissa was already walking away, her panic about her friend apparently forgotten now the role had been filled. 'I already have a job at this wedding, remember? I'm in charge of the venue!'

'Then you'd better find someone to take over

for you. You'll be fine,' Melissa called back over her shoulder as she headed back towards the Gatehouse. 'Just do everything I say.'

'Yeah, because that always worked out so well when we were kids,' Eloise grumbled as the front door swung shut. That was how she'd walked in on her mother kissing the first proper, grown-up boyfriend Eloise had ever had, a week before she'd left for university. Because Melissa had sent her down into the prop room at the theatre to re-trieve something or other she obviously didn't re-ally need. Afterwards, Melissa had claimed that she couldn't *possibly* have known that they were down there, but really, wasn't it all for Eloise's own good anyway? She'd practically done her a favour...especially since everyone had been talk-ing about them for weeks behind Eloise's back. Melissa had truly believed that she'd done the right thing sending her down there to find out the truth for herself.

And maybe she had. She'd certainly cemented Eloise's decision to never trust another actor. If only she'd also warned her about business stu-dents.

Maid of honour for Melissa Sommers. How

on earth had this happened? And the worst part was—

'Sounds like we'll be spending even more time together.' Noah's voice was warm, deep and far too close to her ear.

Eloise sighed. That. That was the worst thing. Because the maid of honour was *expected* to pair up with the best man, and that would not make her resolution to stay away from Noah Cross any easier at all.

She turned and found him standing directly behind her, close enough that if she'd stepped back a centimetre or two she'd have been in his arms. Suddenly she was glad he'd alerted her to his presence with his words.

She shifted further away and tried to look like a professional, instead of a teenager with a crush. Looking up at him, she felt the strange heat flush over her skin again at his gorgeousness. Then she focused, and realised he was frowning.

'Apparently so,' she agreed. 'But I'm sure I'll be far too busy with all the wedding arrangements—'

'Oh, I doubt it,' Noah interrupted, but he still didn't sound entirely happy about the idea, which surprised her. Perhaps she'd misread his flirting earlier. Maybe he really was like that with everyone and, now the reality of having to spend time with her had set in, he was less keen on the idea. 'Melissa has quite the packed schedule for the wedding party, you know. She's right—you're going to have to find someone to take over most of your job here.'

Eloise sighed. She *did* know. She'd helped Laurel plan it, after all.

And, now she thought about it, every last bit of the schedule involved the maid of honour and the best man being together.

Noah smiled, a hint of the charm he'd exhibited earlier showing through despite the frown, and Eloise's heart beat twice in one moment as she accepted the inevitable.

She was doomed.

She had the most ridiculous crush on a man who clearly found her a minor inconvenience.

And—even worse—the whole world was going to be watching, laughing at her pretending that she could live in this world of celebrities, mocking her for thinking she could ever be pretty enough, funny enough…just *enough* for Noah Cross.

Eloise felt the blood drain from her head as she gripped the edge of the reception desk to try and conquer the dizziness that overcame her at the idea.

Ten years on and Melissa Sommers had just delivered her into hell all over again.

Perfect.

CHAPTER FOUR

'YOU LOOK LIKE you need a drink.' In Noah's experience, that was a good line with stressed out women. But in this case it wasn't a line—well, it wasn't *just* a line. Eloise looked as if she might keel over at any moment. Her already pale skin had faded to the same white as the expensive sheets on his four-poster bed and her bright eyes were huge in her face. Most women he knew would have loved to have been tagged to play maid of honour for Melissa Sommers, and few of them would have objected to spending more time with him as best man either.

But Eloise, he was learning quickly, wasn't quite like all the other women he knew.

Maybe he couldn't indulge in the sort of fun he'd planned with her—not if he wanted that part, and he did. But they were going to be spending a lot of time together, it seemed. The least he could do was help her out, and get to know her a bit.

If not in *quite* the way he'd like…

'I'm fine.' Eloise's voice was faint and not at all believable.

'Sure you are.' Noah didn't bother hiding his sarcasm as he took her elbow. 'Look, at least come and sit down for a few minutes.'

'With you?' Eloise's gaze shot to his face, then she shook her head and looked away again. 'I'm working. I can't sit down and I definitely can't drink.'

'Yeah, well, you look like death—no offence. So you kind of need to do something if you don't want to scare the guests.'

Eloise scowled at him, a little colour finally coming back into her cheeks. 'If I'm so terrifying, why aren't I scaring you away?'

'I don't scare easily,' Noah said. 'Haven't you seen all my horror movies?'

'No,' Eloise said, but he was pretty sure she was lying. Maybe she *was* a closet star-struck fan. Except in that case he'd kind of expect her to be nicer to him. 'Look, I'm fine. I just need a moment alone.' She stepped away, towards the other side of the lobby. Noah followed, pausing at her side as she fiddled with the latch on the glass doors that led out to some sort of terrace. 'You don't need to watch me, you know.'

'You're nice to watch,' Noah said with a shrug. Looking was still okay, right? Looking was discreet. He hoped. 'It's not exactly a hardship.'

'I meant…I just need to get some air.'

'Fine by me,' Noah agreed. Then he followed her out onto the terrace, ignoring her heavy sigh.

'What is it with you?' Eloise snapped as he shut the door behind them.

'Me? Nothing at all. You, on the other hand, looked like you were about to pass out, all because some blonde asked you to wear a pretty dress. I mean, I know it's probably stupidly expensive, but still. Formalwear doesn't usually cause fainting fits, in my experience.'

'Yeah, well, clearly you've never experienced formalwear around Melissa Sommers before.' She stalked to the edge of the terrace, leaning on the stone wall as she stared out over the river beyond. Noah gave her a moment then rested his arms beside hers, enjoying the view.

Despite the bitter cold, the air felt fresh on his face, waking him up after a long night of travelling. He felt…alive, somehow, in this place. More alert, more open to the world around him.

Or maybe that was the anticipation of his video call with Stefan, the director of *Eight Days After.* It was strange, but it felt as if that script and this place had become intertwined in his mind, as if being at Morwen Hall would help him become the actor he needed to be to do the part justice.

'Why are you following me around?' Eloise asked eventually, after long moments.

'Honestly? I'm not sure.' Noah shook his head, trying to make sense of it himself. 'There's something about you. The moment I saw you this morning, I wanted…' He broke off.

'I've seen the photos and read the reports,' Eloise said drily. 'I know what your sort wants when it comes to women.' Of course she did. Because, apparently, he wasn't at all discreet about that. He wondered what people would make of the truth— that most of those women on his arm were there to be seen, the same way he was. Often, that was as far as things went.

Noah gave a self-deprecating laugh. 'Reports of my promiscuity may be greatly exaggerated. Besides…that wasn't what I was thinking.'

Colour flooded Eloise's cheeks, the pink clashing with the vibrant flame red of her hair. 'Of course not. I didn't mean...I wasn't assuming that you wanted to...'

Time to put her out of her misery. 'Not because you're not attractive. You're gorgeous.' Her cheeks turned a deeper pink at the compliment. 'And don't get me wrong. I'm totally planning on flirting with you some more later.' If he didn't at least flirt, the world's media would think he was sick or something, and that publicity could be even worse. Maybe.

'You mean you're not now?' If she thought this was flirting, he could have totally snowed her if he had the chance. He sighed at the idea of the lost opportunity.

'Right now, I'm just making sure you're okay. And wondering what the deal is with you and Melissa.'

'*That's* why you're following me around? Because you're nosy?'

'Not *nosy* exactly.' Men weren't nosy, were they? Curious, perhaps. Nosy was for old ladies and people on the neighbourhood watch. 'I just... you intrigue me. And I can't explain why. Except that maybe it has to do with this movie I might be making… Anyway, that doesn't matter. What matters is, I'm interested. I find myself wanting to know more about you, which is unusual for me, I assure you. But, since I do…I'm a good listener, really. If you wanted to talk about why the idea of being Melissa's maid of honour makes you want to throw up or pass out, I'll listen.'

'You mean you'll stand there until I tell you, whether I want to share or not.'

'Basically, yes.'

'Great.' Eloise sighed, then turned to rest her back against the stone wall of the terrace, staring back at him with those big blue-green eyes. 'Fine. You want the whole sob story? I don't know what Melissa Sommers is like on set but when she was a teenager she was a bully, a cheat and she made my life a misery. In fact, part of me wonders if the only reason she's holding her wedding at Morwen Hall—and the only reason she asked her half-sister to be her wedding planner, come to that—is so that she can lord her success over all the little people she left behind. And I know I sound bitter and jealous, but I'm not—really, I'm not. I wouldn't be Melissa for all the tea in

China. But that doesn't mean I'm not allowed to hate her a little bit.'

'I never said it did,' Noah replied, bemused. Where had Eloise been hiding all that anger and all that rage all morning? Ever since he'd arrived, she'd been professional, courteous, distant, and never even the slightest bit inappropriate. He'd been starting to think he might never get under that pale skin. But now it seemed that Eloise had limits—just like everyone else—and Melissa had just passed them.

What had she called Melissa? A bully and a cheat. 'Well, I guess I can see why you don't want to be her maid of honour.'

Eloise gave a watery chuckle and hid her face with her hands. 'It's going to be horrendous.'

'Oh, it won't be that bad.' Noah slung an arm around her slim shoulders for moral support and she stiffened instantly. If she'd felt anything like the tingles that ran up his arm at the contact, he didn't blame her.

That wasn't like it was with all the other women he'd dated either. It seemed nothing about Eloise was usual.

'You'll wear the dress, pose for some photos,

give a couple of short interviews, dance with me...'

Eloise groaned. If he didn't have such a healthy ego, Noah might be starting to take some offence around now.

'You don't like dancing?' he asked.

'I don't like any of it.' Eloise lifted her face and he could see the edge of fear in her eyes. She wasn't exaggerating. Something about the maid of honour job really had her off-balance. 'I hate being the centre of attention.'

'I'm pretty sure that's going to be Melissa, how-ever expensive your frock.'

Eloise shook her head. 'You don't get it. I hate people looking at me. I hate anyone noticing me, noticing what I do.' Which explained her prickly reaction to his attentions, at least. 'You can't understand—your entire life is basically about shouting, "Hey, look at me!" and seeing how many people you can get to turn around.'

'My whole career, a decade of work, reduced to a schoolyard attention grab.' Noah gave an overly dramatic sigh, hoping it might lighten the mood. 'The saddest part is, you're right. But now I've seen the error of my ways, I'll go and become a hotel manager instead.'

'I didn't use to be a hotel manager,' Eloise said, ignoring his attempt at humour. 'I was a chambermaid for years, then worked my way up. My whole career at this hotel has been about fading into the background, not being noticed by the rich and famous who come to stay here. Putting on a show, a spectacle, but not drawing attention to myself. The whole point is that every stay is supposed to go so seamlessly that no one ever notices I'm here, working away in the background.'

Noah couldn't help it; he let out a bark of a laugh. 'The background? Honey, you couldn't fade into the background if you tried.'

Eloise pulled a face. 'I know, I know, the hair stands out.'

'It's not the hair,' Noah said, although that was part of it. 'It's you. Your beauty. That would stand out anywhere.' At least, it did to him. Although, maybe that was just because he knew now that he couldn't have her.

He pulled back, away from Eloise, and strode over towards the doors to the hotel again. It unnerved him, just a little, how easy it was to listen to Eloise talk. How natural his replies felt. How, without even thinking about it, he let in some real feeling between the jokes.

She was looking at him curiously now and he knew he needed to end this moment. People always wanted a secret in return for their own. And he had no intention of giving up any of his.

'You think I'm beautiful?' she asked, her eyes wide and vulnerable, and Noah swore silently in his head.

Because she meant it. He could tell that much straight away. This wasn't the usual coyness of a Hollywood actress, or the 'I'm a model but still don't believe I'm pretty' type of false insecurity. She was honestly surprised.

'I can't be the only person to tell you that,' he said, searching for a way out. Because that lack of self-awareness, that would be his undoing. He'd only known one other person so artlessly unaware of her own beauty.

Sally.

And he really wasn't thinking about her any more this weekend. It had been seven years, for goodness' sake.

'No, but you're the first movie star to say it,'

Eloise said, and the moment was broken. Because he'd never been a movie star to Sally. He'd just been her best friend.

But to Eloise he was Noah Cross, the brand—and that was all he needed to be. She didn't need to see any deeper, and he didn't need to worry about having to let her in too far. He just had to keep his eye on the prize—his name in that little golden envelope when they announced the coveted award for Best Actor, once *Eight Days After* came out.

And all he had to do to achieve that was not sleep with Eloise, and knock his audition out of the park.

At least one of those should be no trouble at all. He just wished he could be entirely sure which one.

Eloise let herself back into the hotel, her dizziness faded but replaced by a strange confusion after the unexpected interlude with Noah on the terrace. At least he'd retreated up to his room to let her recover her wits in peace. She couldn't cope with any more of that intense conversation and gaze right now.

What had all that been about? She'd expected to get hit on by sex-crazed or drunk actors looking for a fling at the wedding—it happened often enough while working at the hotel, however much she tried to fade into the background. The rich and famous, in her experience, seemed to expect to be able to seduce anyone they wanted. And actors were the worst—they were all about the quick, meaningless fling. Which was still better than the times they pretended it was something more, that they'd fallen for her charms at first sight and couldn't live without her in their beds.

She knew better than to believe them. Her mother had been the queen of that game, and look how that had ended up.

No, she knew actors, knew the entitled clientele of Morwen Hall, and she knew how they behaved.

Noah Cross was not living up to the stereotype and it bothered her.

Of course there were probably *some* actors and actresses who managed to stay happily married and faithful, or who were looking for long-term love. She'd just never met any of them. Or seen them in the celebrity magazines in the staff-room. And she'd *never* expect Noah Cross, famed ladies' man, to be one of them.

In fairness, she had no evidence that he was. He'd admitted he was flirting with her—even if he didn't seem inclined to take it any further.

Either way, he hadn't gone about it the way she'd expected. She'd expected the flattery, the lusty looks, the charm. She hadn't expected him to ask questions about her history with Melissa, or to show such concern for her well-being.

Actually, he'd seemed pretty surprised by that too, so maybe this was a new thing for him.

The main doors opened again and Laurel burst through, followed closely by a guy who looked a lot like Riley.

Very closely.

Eloise narrowed her eyes as the man rested a hand on Laurel's waist, and Laurel jumped with surprise. There was definitely something weird going on here.

Pushing thoughts of Noah's weirdness out of her head, Eloise covered the lobby in long strides, ready to decipher Laurel's weirdness instead.

'Hey. You're back!'

Laurel's smile seemed a little forced. 'I am.'

'And you brought company.' Eloise's gaze flicked up to the man with his hand on Laurel. He really did look an awful lot like Riley. Which probably meant...

'Eloise, this is Dan. Riley's brother.' Of course. But that didn't explain his and Laurel's closeness. 'Dan, this is Eloise. She's the manager of Morwen Hall.'

'Pleased to meet you,' Dan said, placing the shopping bag he was carrying on the ground and holding out his hand.

'Acting Manager,' Eloise corrected automatically, as she took it and shook. The title wasn't hers yet—and wouldn't be unless this wedding went off without a hitch.

'Not for long,' Laurel said, and this time her smile seemed real. 'So, what's been happening here?'

'Cassidy, the maid of honour, has taken a fall while skiing and broken her leg, so her husband is bringing his mistress to the wedding instead.'

Also, I seem to have an odd connection with the best man that makes me want to tear his clothes off, even though he's the sort of man I despise, and he seems more interested in getting to know me.

Maybe she'd save that information for later, when she and Laurel were able to grab a moment alone. She needed to talk to *someone* about it.

Laurel's mouth fell into an open O shape, her eyes almost as wide. 'So Melissa doesn't have a maid of honour?'

Eloise winced. 'Not exactly. She's making me do it.'

She hadn't thought Laurel's eyes could get any wider but her response to this information proved her wrong. 'You poor, poor thing.'

At least she didn't have to worry about Melissa's half-sister being offended she hadn't been chosen. That was something, Eloise supposed. 'Yeah. I'm thrilled, as you can imagine. And it means I'll have to call in my deputy to cover for me at the hotel this week. He will *not* be thrilled. I can probably keep on top of the wedding events at least, so he only has to deal with the guests.' She sighed. 'What about you? How did the favours go?'

And what's the deal with you and your future half-brother-in-law?

'Fine, they're all sorted.' Laurel waved her hand towards the large glossy shopping bag that Dan had picked up again. 'Then I got Dan's car to pick me up on the way back.'

'That was…convenient.' Eloise stared rather pointedly at where Dan's hand was *still* resting on Laurel's waist, and the petite wedding planner blushed.

'Um, yes. Actually, I meant to tell you… Dan and I…'

'So I see,' Eloise said when Laurel appeared at a loss for how to finish that statement.

'We had sort of been keeping it under wraps,' Dan said, pulling Laurel closer to his side. Laurel stiffened for a moment then relaxed against him, her cheeks a little pink. 'What with the wedding and everything. Didn't want to steal Melissa's thunder, you know? But now the secret's out anyway…'

'This is brilliant!' Eloise burst out, the answer to at least one of her problems coming to her in a flash. Laurel looked a little startled at Eloise's sudden enthusiasm, at least until she explained. 'Melissa has insisted on Riley staying in a separate room until the wedding night, so I had to give him Dan's—sorry, Dan.' She gave Riley's brother a quick smile. 'But if you two are together, then that's fine because you'll be sharing anyway!'

'Sharing…right.' Laurel's smile had frozen into that sort of rictus again.

Eloise frowned. 'As long as that's okay…?'

'Of course!' Laurel said, too brightly. 'I mean, why wouldn't we?'

'Exactly,' Dan said, not looking quite as certain as Eloise might have expected either. 'Why wouldn't we?'

They were looking at each other now, not Eloise, staring into each other's eyes. Eloise definitely got the feeling she was intruding on a moment.

Quizzing Laurel on exactly *when* she'd found the time to go falling for Riley's brother would have to wait until she could get her alone. For now, she'd just chalk it up to fate and cross one more thing off her epic to-do list. At least now she could get on with the next thing on that list— the welcome drinks.

'Well, I'm glad that's all sorted,' she said, clapping her hands together in the hope it might bring Laurel and Dan back to the present.

It didn't. Eloise gave up.

'See you both later, then,' she said, and headed upstairs to her room to change into something more suitable for a maid of honour to wear while resisting flirting with the best man.

CHAPTER FIVE

'THAT IS A very boring dress,' Noah said as he handed Eloise a flute of champagne. He'd been watching her since he'd arrived at the bar for the welcome drinks, and she hadn't welcomed a single drink yet. She had to be desperate for one. He knew he was.

He'd intended to stay away from Eloise this evening, despite his promise of a flirtation earlier. Tessa had sent him a pointed text message saying she hoped he was behaving himself, as she had a call booked in with Stefan about the audition. Clearly she was serious about this, and so he would be too.

But then he'd spent an hour making small talk with the other wedding guests and, by the end of it, he was desperate for a conversation with somebody who had never even wanted to be in a film. Which, at Melissa's wedding, basically left Eloise.

When had this sort of event grown so meaningless? All industry chatter and gossip, and nothing of any substance. Unlike Eloise's boring black shift dress which, in his opinion, had far too much substance. It could have done with a little bit of sheer fabric somewhere, or even just a little less weight. It hung over her body like a sack. Eloise's body, Noah had decided from watching her move around the room, needed the sort of fabric that flowed, that moved with her, showing off her long, lean lines and gentle curves.

From the way Eloise was scowling at him, he guessed she disagreed. Oh, well. He was getting used to it.

'I didn't realise we'd reached the stage in our acquaintance where you felt comfortable insulting my fashion sense.'

'I like to skip ahead to the good parts. Why waste time on the small talk?' He flashed her his most charming smile and she just rolled her eyes.

Eloise Miller was going to be a challenge to win over—especially if he wasn't allowed to seduce her. Fortunately, Noah loved challenges.

'Well, you'll get to see me in the hideous concoction Melissa has chosen for the bridesmaids soon enough,' she assured him, then raised the champagne flute to her lips to take a sip. 'Hopefully, that will be an interesting enough dress to keep you satisfied.'

Noah had a feeling that whatever dress Melissa had picked, it wouldn't be anywhere near enough to satisfy him. Even standing beside Eloise, just watching her cool, pale skin and her blazing hair, he felt too warm, as if he might get burnt if he touched her. But that didn't stop his whole body aching to reach out anyway. What was it about this woman? She wasn't even trying—and he'd had enough women try with him to know—and yet she kept pulling him into her orbit, keeping him tethered there until it was physically hard to pull away.

The room was filled with beautiful women, yet the only one he could see was Eloise.

And that was going to be a problem. Because he really couldn't sleep with her. He was being discreet—and that definitely meant no public fling with the maid of honour.

'I'm sure the bridesmaids' dresses will be lovely,' he lied, trying not to imagine Eloise in something slippery, something low-cut, something that just fell off her skin as he pushed it aside…

'No, you're not,' Eloise cut into his thoughts. 'You know as well as I do that Melissa will have chosen something designed to make *her* look even more beautiful. Which, given the A-list beauty status of the rest of her bridesmaids, means that we'll all be wearing sackcloth and ashes, or whatever the modern wedding equivalent is. In this case, something in blue-green satin and chiffon, I believe.'

'You'd look good in anything,' Noah replied without thinking, and she looked at him with wide eyes.

'Thank you,' she said, sounding surprised. 'But I'd reserve judgement until you've seen the dress, if I were you. Melissa is not above using her powers of fashion for evil.'

They stood side by side, observing the room, and Noah wondered if she was supposed to be working, doing something, instead of standing here with him. Then he wondered if, actually, he was meant to be doing something, in his capacity as best man. Then he decided he didn't care. He was exactly where he wanted to be.

'Did you know about those two?' Eloise nodded across the room to where the little wedding planner and Riley's brother were talking with the parents of the groom. As they chatted, Dan reached out and rested his hand at the small of Laurel's back and she leant against him, apparently finding strength and support in his nearness.

For a moment Noah couldn't help but think that looked nice, having that sort of connection. And then he remembered the price and shook the thought away.

'No. They're together?' *That* hadn't come up in any of the emails and schedules Laurel had been sending over for months.

'Apparently.' Eloise's gaze didn't move from the group across the room, but Noah couldn't be sure if she was watching Laurel and Dan or taking in Melissa's mother's thunderous face. It looked as if someone else hadn't known about the relationship either. He wondered if the bride knew yet… That could be interesting, when she arrived. Melissa believed in making an entrance, and that required being fashionably late. 'I don't know if it's serious. I mean…it's not like Melissa and Riley, is it? Another showbiz marriage destined to fail.'

'Not all marriages end in divorce,' Noah said mildly. 'Only, like, half. Maybe three-quarters, in Hollywood.'

The look Eloise gave him was scathing. 'That's a rousing argument for the institution of marriage.'

He shrugged. 'It's not really my thing.'

'Yeah, I get that.' She tilted her head a little to the side as she considered him. Noah tried not to shift from one foot to the other, giving away his discomfort. Usually, he was used to being scrutinised from the other side of a camera or a screen. Up close and personal, it felt a little invasive. As if Eloise was looking deeper than he wanted her to know existed. 'So, how did Riley rope you into being best man, then? You guys must be pretty close, I guess.'

'Not really,' Noah admitted, glad the focus had shifted away from him and onto Melissa and Riley for a while. Their wedding was a much safer topic. 'I mean, we've made a few movies together, done the press junkets. But that's about it.'

'Huh.' She was looking again. Studying him.

'What?' Noah shifted his weight from one foot to the other and swapped his empty champagne flute for a full one as a waiter passed.

'I just figured…the way they both talked about you when we were doing the planning—especially Riley—I figured you were a bigger part of their lives.'

'Riley said that? I mean, he made it sound that way?' He'd always assumed that Melissa had insisted on Riley asking him, purely for the celebrity cachet that came with having Noah Cross as best man. But maybe he'd been wrong. After all, as his agent had pointed out, he wasn't always the best at connecting with people on a deeper level. Even his friends.

'Yeah. He did.'

'I…I don't usually like to get too close to people I work with,' Noah said, wondering why he felt as if he needed to make excuses to this woman. It was her eyes, he decided. The way they seemed to look right into his soul—assuming he still had one after a decade in Hollywood. He was pretty sure some of the women he'd dated would claim otherwise.

'Or anyone else,' Eloise suggested.

Noah tried to ignore her remark but, seeing as it came so soon after Tessa's comments on the phone, he couldn't help himself from asking, 'What makes you say that?'

'I've seen the photos,' Eloise said with a shrug. 'All those pictures of you with a different woman every week. Not exactly the hallmark of a guy who gets up close and personal. At least, not in the non-physical sense.'

She sounded too casual as she said it, too desperate for him to believe she didn't care what he did with women. And, on less than twelve hours' acquaintance, why would she?

But she did. Noah was almost certain of it.

And he couldn't do a single thing about it.

'There's nothing wrong with having a little fun,' he said lightly, watching her face carefully to read her response. 'As long as everyone involved knows that's exactly what it is.'

'Just fun. Casual. Meaningless. Shallow.' She met his gaze with her own fierce blue-green eyes. How was it she seemed to see right inside him, yet he couldn't read her at all? He prided himself on his ability to decipher people—to read enough to understand them without ever needing to get too close. But Eloise was a mystery.

Noah hated mysteries.

'That's right.' He moved a little closer, slowly, so as not to spook her. Just enough that the sleeve of his jacket brushed against her bare arm.

She flinched.

He was right. She cared, for some reason. His inability to even contemplate monogamy bothered her, and he could not begin to understand why.

But he intended to find out. If he understood her, maybe he'd stop being so obsessed with her—stop feeling the need to be near her, to question her, to deepen their acquaintance. Because deep and meaningful was the last thing he wanted, with any woman. Whatever Tessa said.

Eloise's tongue flicked over her lips as she raised her eyes to his then looked away again.

Perhaps he was making this too complicated. Maybe Eloise's problem had nothing to do with deeper motivations at all.

Perhaps she just wanted him the same way he wanted her.

And if that was the case he had an even bigger problem.

He had to be sure.

'A fling is always good for making a wedding a little more entertaining, don't you find?' he asked, and watched her cheeks turn pink.

Gotcha.

She wanted him. And he *really* wanted her.

Okay, so he couldn't have her. But that didn't mean he couldn't play a little. Just to keep in practice.

He could find out exactly what issues she had that stopped her from even contemplating a bit of fun. He might even get her to lighten up a bit.

It would be his good deed for the day or something.

Even Tessa would have to approve of that. Right?

He was flirting with her.

Noah Cross, Hollywood heart-throb and womaniser extraordinaire, was flirting with her.

She hadn't been sure earlier, couldn't quite tell if his easy charm was just something he pulled out for all the ladies. Sure, it felt personal and attentive and tingly—no, not tingly. She didn't do tingly. Anyway. She hadn't been one hundred per cent certain that his flirtatiousness had anything to do with *her* exactly. He could have been like that with every woman he met for all she knew. In fact, he probably was.

But this, now; this was personal. Focused. He was staring deep into her eyes, as if he hoped to find the meaning of life there—or at least a way into her underwear.

Well. Noah Cross was going to be sorely disappointed.

'I've never had a fling at a wedding,' she said, purposefully omitting the 'before' from the end of the sentence. 'Before' implied she was thinking about doing it this time, and she wasn't.

Oh, all right, she was. Any straight woman with a pulse would at least *think* about it if Noah Cross propositioned her, she was sure. But thinking was as far as Eloise was willing to go.

'Don't you think you should give it a try? Just once?' Noah leaned in a little closer. 'How else will you know if you like it or not?'

Eloise pulled back, fixing him with her sternest manager stare. This would all be so much easier if her whole body didn't hum at the very sight of him. 'And who, exactly, are you suggesting I have this fling with?'

Noah attempted a self-effacing look, which—kudos to his skill as an actor—almost looked realistic. 'Well, there is always that old tradition about the maid of honour and the best man. But really, the whole room is full of attractive men—or women, if that's your thing. All of them famous and at least half of them single—or acting as if they are, anyway.'

'I don't date actors,' she said, the response as automatic and instinctive as saying yes to a cup of tea. 'And I definitely don't have meaningless flings with them.' That wasn't who she was. She'd worked hard to shake off the assumptions people in this town had made about her, based on her family and her upbringing. She wasn't about to abandon her reputation now for one night with a movie star, just because he made her body respond in ways she'd forgotten it could.

Except he'd only offered himself as one possibility, hadn't he? Clearly he wasn't overly invested in this flirtation. It was all probably just a game to him. To get the repressed hotel manager to cut loose and go wild.

Well, not her. Not a chance.

'Never?' Noah raised his eyebrows. 'Wow. What did we poor, defenceless actors ever do to you?'

'Not to me. I told you. I don't date actors.' It was *technically* true—Derek hadn't been an actor when she'd started dating him. He'd been a director. But then the leading man had fallen sick and he'd taken on the role—starring opposite Eloise's mother. And from there it had been an old, familiar story.

She didn't want to get into what so many actors had done to her mother. Or, more to the point, what her mother had done to them—and, by extension, what she'd done to Eloise and her father. Derek, the boyfriend her mother had stolen from her, had only been one in a long list of leading men she'd seduced then cast aside. If Eloise had needed proof that actors were all the same, she could pull out the box of old programmes her mother had kept from her amateur dramatics days and put together a list of names that made her point for her. And that was just in her home town. How much worse must Hollywood be? She didn't want to find out.

And Noah didn't need to know her sordid history. Especially since she absolutely was not going to sleep with him. No matter how much she wanted to.

A waiter passed and Eloise grabbed another glass of champagne. Melissa was paying for it, and it was her fault that Eloise had found herself in this position in the first place.

'So, you've never dated an actor but you hate us all indiscriminately anyway. Interesting.' Noah leant back against the bar behind him. 'Care to tell me why you cling onto this prejudice so tenaciously? Especially since we've established that any fling at this wedding won't be happening between us?'

He wasn't the sort to give up—Eloise knew that after only a day in his company. If she had to guess, she'd say that Noah was the sort of guy who liked to understand something well enough for his own purposes and then move on. He was only interested in the surface knowledge, enough to fake a part, she supposed.

Well, surface she could do. She just didn't want

to get down to the deep, painful memories that lay underneath it.

Of course, she was pretty sure Noah didn't want to either. If she actually broke down and gave him her sob story, he'd run in the other direction. That was something to keep in reserve, in case she needed it.

'You're all the same,' she said with a shrug. 'You fall in love for the length of time it takes to get a movie made, or to star in a play. Then, once it's all over, you're onto the next leading lady or love interest. Half your relationships are film promo, as far as I can tell.'

Noah raised his eyebrows. 'Wow. You really do have a chip on your shoulder about this.'

'Tell me I'm wrong,' Eloise challenged. 'You said yourself you were just looking for a fling.'

'There's nothing wrong with a fling, as long as both parties know what they're getting into,' Noah said mildly.

'Which is what, exactly?' Of course he'd think that. It was the perfect justification for never having to have a real relationship. 'A meaningless encounter with someone you never really get to know?'

'What's so wrong with that?' Noah asked with a shrug. 'Maybe we're not supposed to know the innermost depths of *everyone* we meet.'

'Perhaps not. But…don't you want that connection?' Eloise had to admit she did. Which might be the reason she didn't date so much. She hadn't met many guys over the past few years she wanted to get to know that well. But that sounded a bit too much like conceding the point, so she didn't say it.

'Real and deep doesn't mean for ever, Eloise.' There was a harshness to Noah's voice she hadn't heard before. 'The most real and important relationship of my life lasted barely twenty-four hours.'

She blinked. That was definitely new. 'That must have been…intense.' She couldn't imagine it. From his tone she could tell that, whatever the relationship was, it had mattered—and mattered deeply. She couldn't imagine how it must have felt to have that and then have it taken away again. What had happened? She wanted to ask but, before she could find a way to phrase the question, Noah spoke again.

'It was.' He flashed her a smile that was so

at odds with the conversation Eloise wondered for a moment if she'd missed the joke. 'Enough for one lifetime, anyway. Which is why I prefer things my way these days—fun, light and easy.'

'And never getting in too deep,' Eloise said, frowning.

'That way you don't drown,' Noah joked. 'I know when I'm out of my depth.'

She wanted to ask more, wanted to try and understand his attitude. Not to understand Noah himself, exactly, she realised, but to try and get some perspective on her mother. Was this how she'd felt? Or had she just been incapable of real love, as Eloise had always believed?

Maybe Noah was too. In which case, it was just as well she had no intention of getting any closer to him. A fling might be his sort of thing, but it wasn't hers. It never had been.

And she was firmly ignoring the small voice at the back of her head whispering, *How will you know if you never try it?* Especially as it sounded exactly like Noah Cross.

'So, who was she?' Eloise asked, but Noah wasn't listening any more. And, as she followed his gaze to the doorway, Eloise forgot what she'd been asking about.

Melissa stood in the entrance, arms wide, wearing a stunning forest-green gown that left her shoulders and a great deal of cleavage bare, before nipping in at her waist and following every curve down to her knees, where it flared out again.

'Now *that* is not a boring dress,' Noah murmured. 'Of course, it would look better on you.'

'Liar.' Melissa looked as if she'd been born to wear that dress, and the smile on her face said she knew it.

'It's true.' Noah pressed up behind her as the crowd gathered around the bride. 'You have the height to pull it off—your legs would look endless. And that colour…made for a redhead.'

'Maybe.' But she'd never have the confidence to wear it. Not in a million years.

'Of course, you'd have to wear your hair down,' Noah added, touching the hundreds of pins that kept her hair firmly out of her way when she was working. 'Which would be an added bonus.'

Clearly the guy had a thing for redheads. Which was funny because she'd never seen him with any on the red carpet.

'I thought we'd established that we weren't going to be having any sort of fling,' she said drily. 'I'm pretty sure that means you can stop with the compliments now.'

Noah shrugged. 'I figured we could be friends instead. Friends compliment each other.'

Did they? Eloise wasn't sure she'd know. But that might just be because Melissa had always been her baseline for friendship.

'Friends?'

'Yeah,' he said. 'Friends. Think you can manage it?'

'I'll give it a try,' she replied drily. Friends with another Hollywood star. Hopefully this one would go better than her friendship with Melissa.

'Everyone! My fiancé and I are just so delighted to welcome you all here to celebrate our wedding.' Melissa beamed around the room and Riley stepped out of her shadow, looking awkward in a dinner jacket, and gave a little wave. 'I hope you all have just the best time—' She cut off abruptly, her smile replaced by a sudden scowl.

Eloise tried to figure out what had changed, and followed Melissa's gaze to…oh, dear.

Dan had his arm around Laurel and, from

where Eloise stood, she could see him staring up at Melissa, a challenge in his eyes.

'What the *hell* is going on here?' Melissa asked, her hands on her hips.

'Guess we weren't the only ones who didn't know about Laurel and Dan,' Noah murmured as Eloise headed into the fray to smooth over the situation.

Playtime was over.

Noah sighed, putting the script to one side again, and wished that the curtains of the four-poster bed didn't feel as if they were closing in. He had shut them to try and give himself a cosy cocoon in which to read through the script for *Eight Days After* again, looking for those deeper resonances he knew he'd need to hit to get the part. But instead he just felt trapped.

Maybe Tessa was right. Maybe this wasn't the part for him. He was a good actor, he knew that. But this role…maybe it cut a little too close to home.

He thought back over his conversation with Eloise. Now there was a woman who believed in deep and meaningful. He almost wished he could just get her to explain it to him, so he could fake it well enough to get the part without ever actually having to feel it himself. If there was a woman in the world who could do it, Noah would place money on it being Eloise. There was something about her eyes, her expressions. The way everything she felt or thought was telegraphed out to her audience in her face. He could almost see the thoughts floating across her eyes, like subtitles on a foreign movie.

She didn't think much of him—that was certain. Which was a shame, given his body's automatic reaction whenever she was near—but also probably just as well, under the circumstances.

No, it was just as well they'd established the 'no fling' ground rules. Not only was he not in the market for it right now, but she was clearly out for love, marriage, the whole shebang. And he most definitely wasn't. Noah wasn't the sort of guy who'd let a girl carry those sorts of hopes into bed with her, even if it was the only way to get her there. It wasn't fair and it wasn't worth it. He was always very clear about what he was willing to offer.

And he'd only ever offered more once. Only to have it all taken away twenty-four hours later.

Suddenly restless, Noah pushed the curtains aside and jumped off the bed, heading for the minibar.

He shouldn't have mentioned Sally to Eloise. Oh, he might not have said her name, might not have gone into detail, but Eloise was the sort of woman who asked questions. She'd want to know more and, given how much time they were likely to be spending together over the next few days, she'd try her hardest to find out. Noah foresaw a lot of time spent sidestepping questions in his future. Good job he'd had all that fancy media training. Avoiding Eloise's questions would be as hard as any interview he'd ever sat.

He supposed he'd started it. He'd wanted to play, wanted to pick at her secrets and truths. It was only fair she got to do the same in return.

Noah poured a healthy measure of whisky into one of the glass tumblers on top of the well-stocked refrigerator, then bypassed the sofa to head back to the bed, leaving the curtains open this time. He took a sip, savouring the burn of the alcohol in his throat. This was what he needed to focus on—the here and now, the current moment. Not a woman seven years dead, or the future he had lost that day.

Eloise might think that all actors were only in it for the cheap thrill, the quick, meaningless satisfaction. But she was wrong. He'd wanted more once—and he'd had it too.

Just not for very long.

He'd spent his whole teenage years in love with one woman. And when she finally realised she might feel the same…he'd let her down, just when she'd needed him most.

He knew how it felt to have his heart ripped from his chest, and he wasn't about to go seeking that again.

He took another gulp of whisky. He didn't need the memories tonight. He needed to focus on the script and how to fake those deeper emotions he'd locked away inside the day Sally died. Because he had no intention of ever feeling them again.

CHAPTER SIX

IT HADN'T TAKEN much to convince Melissa that making a scene about her half-sister and brother-in-law-to-be getting together at her own wedding wasn't the best PR plan she'd ever had, especially with the reporter covering the wedding watching. Melissa had looked stormy for a moment, then reverted to the sweetness and light actress the rest of the room—those who didn't actually know her very well—were expecting. It was almost disconcerting to see the shift, Eloise thought.

Still, she hadn't felt confident leaving Melissa alone with Laurel until the crowd of guests had mostly departed to their beds. Noah had called it quits some time earlier, whispering a goodnight in her ear as he left.

Eloise had spent more of the night remembering the feel of his lips so close to her than she would ever admit to him. By the time morning rolled around, she hadn't had nearly as much sleep as she'd hoped to get.

Yawning, she stretched and reached for her smartphone, sitting on her bedside table. They had another big day ahead of them—especially with the Frost Fair that afternoon. Melissa had wanted something wintry, magical and British for her guests to enjoy as a pre-wedding event. Eloise and Laurel had come up with the idea of a traditional Frost Fair, like they used to hold on the frozen River Thames back in the seventeenth and eighteenth centuries. If nothing else, it would provide quite a spectacle, Eloise was sure.

Of course, first she had to get through a dress fitting with Melissa.

Pressing the screen on her phone, Eloise called Laurel to check on her plans for the day, and quickly checked in with her deputy about anything that might come up while she was being fitted for her maid of honour dress. Laurel, Eloise couldn't help but note, sounded far grumpier than Eloise would if she'd spent the night with a guy as gorgeous as Dan. She hoped that Melissa's reaction the night before hadn't caused prob-

lems between the two of them. Laurel deserved
a nice guy.

Eventually, she couldn't put it off any longer.
Showered and dressed in a knitted navy dress
and knee boots, Eloise headed down to the con-
ference room they'd put aside for the final dress
fittings that morning. Melissa was already there,
holding court over the two other bridesmaids
while a harried-looking woman unpacked pins
and measuring tapes and dress bags.

'And here's the replacement maid of honour,'
Melissa said, looking up as Eloise entered the
room. 'I hope you didn't eat too many of the
canapés last night, Eloise, or you'll never fit into
the dress!' The bridesmaids both laughed, and
Eloise bit her tongue to keep from responding.
Apparently Melissa had already forgotten her
comments about Cassidy, the previous maid of
honour, putting on weight for a part. She'd probably remember in time to make another joke at
Eloise's expense, once she had the dress on.

She really hadn't missed Melissa at all in the
past decade, Eloise thought.

'We were just talking about how Laurel and

Dan tried to steal my thunder last night,' Melissa went on.

'And failed,' one of the bridesmaids, who Eloise faintly recognised from her most recent cinema trip, said. Was she Iona? Eloise wasn't sure. After a while, all those Hollywood blondes started to look the same to her.

'Of course they did!' said the other bridesmaid, who Eloise was almost certain was called Caitlin. 'As if anyone cared about anything except how fabulous Mel looked in that dress last night.'

They all turned to Eloise, apparently waiting for her agreement. 'It was a very beautiful dress,' she said, hoping that was good enough. From what she'd overheard, plenty of people had an opinion on the groom's brother and bride's sister getting together. Some were even giving odds on their relationship outlasting Melissa and Riley's.

'And so is yours!' Melissa clapped her hands together as the seamstress pulled the first bridesmaid's dress from its bag. 'Not as gorgeous as mine, of course, but still. What do you think?'

Eloise stared at the icy blue-green concoction of chiffon and silk. The colour wasn't one she'd ever choose to wear but it was very appropriate for a winter wedding, she supposed. If they insisted on having photos taken outside, her skin colour might actually match the dress. That would be nice.

'It's lovely,' she lied, as she got a good look at the laces at the back of the corset top. Corsets were for people with curves, weren't they? And she didn't have nearly as many of those as Melissa, or the bridesmaids. Eloise had height, long legs and a slender body, none of which, she imagined, were going to be shown off to their best advantage by this dress.

Which shouldn't bother her at all. This was effectively a job, and she wore boring grey suits to work every day and never worried about whether they complemented her complexion. Why should she care now?

Because you'll be standing next to Noah Cross.

She wished she could pretend that she just wanted to look good in the world's media when the photos came out but, given that she was starring in this wedding alongside people who'd made the top ten in the world's most beautiful people list, there wasn't a hope of that to start with.

No, what she was really thinking about were

Noah's words the night before. 'That is a very boring dress.' Even though they'd established there would be no romance between them, a small part of her couldn't help but wish the dress Melissa had picked might have wowed him, just a little.

She sighed. He'd just have to deal with a non-boring but faintly hideous dress, she supposed.

Stepping behind the screen they'd set up, Eloise slipped into the dress and pulled the corset top up over her non-existent curves.

'Let me tighten that for you,' the seamstress said, coming up behind her and yanking on the laces. Eloise winced as all the air flew out of her body. Apparently someone was determined for her to have curves, even if breathing had to be sacrificed.

Once she was suitably tightened and tied, Eloise stepped out into the main room, where the other two bridesmaids were already in their dresses. Apparently actresses didn't have the same privacy issues as normal people. On each of them, the icy blue looked stunning against their blonde hair, and their delicate curves, quite possibly emphasised by breast implants, were highlighted to perfection. Looking at them, Eloise was surer than ever that Melissa's comment about Laurel's cleavage not fitting in the dress was just another excuse not to make her half-sister maid of honour.

'Well, don't you look…?' Melissa trailed off and gave her a patronisingly encouraging smile. 'I told you the dress would fit, didn't I? Corsets are marvellously forgiving.'

'I'll just need to let down the hem a little…' The seamstress fussed around her with the measuring tape.

Eloise wanted nothing more than to strip the dress off right there, no matter who was watching, and get back to hiding in her professional grey suit.

But then she heard Noah's voice from the door to her left. 'Wow.'

Fixing a smile onto her face, she turned to look at him, hoping against hope that he was a good enough actor to make her feel slightly less like an ugly stepsister in a pantomime.

'You look… Wow.' Noah's gaze ran the length of her body before it met her own, and Eloise swallowed as she realised he wasn't acting. Or if he was he was a lot better at it than his films suggested.

'Noah Cross lost for words,' Melissa said, her light tone sounding forced. 'I never thought I'd see the day.'

Noah broke away from staring at her, and Eloise tried to take a deep breath to recover from the intensity of his gaze. Then she remembered the corset and settled for a few shallow ones instead.

'Melissa, I don't think you know how to pick a boring dress.' He said it like a compliment and, from the way Melissa's cheeks turned pink, it might have been the nicest thing he'd ever said to her. But Eloise felt a small glow inside her, knowing that he was making a private joke, just for her, and that Melissa would never get it.

'I'm glad you approve,' she said, apparently placated. 'Now, are you ready to teach your pupil her steps?'

'Steps?' Eloise asked as Melissa and Noah both turned to look at her. She didn't like the sound of that at all.

'For the first dance at the reception,' Melissa explained. 'Obviously, it'll just be Riley and me on the dance floor to start with, but then we've planned for the best man and maid of honour to join us, followed by Iona and Caitlin and their partners. Didn't Laurel mention it?'

'It didn't come up,' Eloise said, her voice faint. She'd been far more concerned with the details of the catering and the rooms than what was actually going to happen at the wedding reception itself. Speeches and dances and so on were Laurel's department, not hers.

At least, they had been.

'It's not a complicated dance,' Noah said, obviously trying to be reassuring. But he didn't get it. It wasn't the steps that bothered her. It wasn't even being in Noah's arms and having to restrain herself from kissing him, hard though that might be. No, it was all the eyes that would be on her as she stepped out onto the dance floor that made her hands shake and her knees wobble. It was being the centre of attention. That was what caused that big ball of anxiety in her chest to double in size.

'Just try your best,' Melissa said, her voice dripping false sympathy. 'Everyone will know you're not a professional, so they won't be expecting much.'

'Well, that's okay then,' Eloise ground out between her clenched teeth.

'Why don't we go practise somewhere else?' Noah suggested, looking between them. 'Far away.'

'Good idea,' Eloise said, stepping back behind the screen to get out of the ridiculous dress in a hurry.

'Oh, I think it would be much better to do it here,' Melissa said as Eloise tugged on the corset strings. 'After all, Eloise might need someone to show her how it's really done. And really, Eloise, I think you'd better keep the dress on. You want to know how it feels to dance in costume, don't you?'

Eloise gave up the unequal fight with the corset strings. Apparently it was time to dance.

Noah stood awkwardly in the middle of the room, waiting for Eloise to join him. She'd stepped back out from behind the screen at Melissa's request, her face red and mutinous.

'Shoes!' Melissa jumped up and dashed across the room, a blur of blonde as she reached into one of four boxes laid out on the table under the window. 'What size are you, Eloise?'

'A seven,' she said, still not looking at Noah, or Melissa, or anywhere that wasn't the floor.

Somehow, Noah got the distinct impression that Eloise wasn't looking forward to dancing with him.

'Cassidy is a six, but I'm sure you'll be able to squeeze into them, won't you?' Melissa smiled sweetly as she handed over the shoes, and Noah prepared to dive in and separate them if Eloise finally lost the last scraps of her composure.

She didn't. Instead, she looked at the shoes in her hand and pulled a face.

'They have ribbons.'

'I know! Aren't they beautiful?' Melissa squealed. Noah hadn't really sensed 'beautiful' from Eloise's tone. 'Go on, put them on. You'll want to practice the dance in them.'

'I don't want to practice the dance at all,' Eloise muttered as she bent to put on the shoes, but Melissa ignored her.

It took some effort, even Noah could see that, but eventually the shoes were on, ribbons tied, and Eloise was proclaimed ready to dance.

'Now, it's a nice simple waltz, really,' Melissa said. 'I'll tell you what, I'll demonstrate with Noah so you can see what Riley and I will be doing. Then you can step in and give it a go.'

Melissa moved into his arms before Noah could agree to the plan, and Iona started up the music. The familiar theme tune from Melissa's biggest movie so far rang out through the room and, over her shoulder, Noah saw Eloise roll her eyes. He smirked at her and she returned the smile, her cheeks finally back to their normal colour.

'Noah! You missed your cue.' Melissa stamped one dainty foot on the floor and Iona started the music once again. 'It's just as well we're rehearsing today. Obviously you haven't been practising on your own.'

'Every morning for twenty minutes, just like you asked, Mel. I swear,' Noah lied shamelessly. It was a waltz. He'd learned how to waltz for his sister's wedding when he was eight. If he could do it then he could do it now.

This time, he hit his cue perfectly, sweeping Melissa around the floor easily. But his attention wasn't on his dance partner. It was on Eloise, watching from the sidelines. Her cheeks might no longer be bright red with embarrassment, but with every bar of the music she grew stiller and smaller somehow, fading away in that ice-blue dress.

That dress. When he'd walked in and seen it, it had blown him away. For all that he'd been spending the last twenty-four hours staring at Eloise, he'd not had a chance to see her in anything that accentuated her figure so well. Even the colour, which he wouldn't have picked for her, added a strange otherworldliness coupled with her blazing hair. She looked like some mythical princess of ice and fire—and utterly unlike the woman who draped herself in shapeless suits and boring black dresses.

But now, as he whirled around the room with Melissa in his arms, she seemed to be retreating back into herself. She'd said she liked to fade into the background, and he hadn't thought it possible. Until he saw her in action.

She'd made herself nothing, and he wanted to drag her out into the light again. Wanted to show her off, to see her beauty reflected around her. Wanted to show *her* how beautiful she was.

But, more than that, he wanted to protect her

from Melissa and whatever plans she had that involved making Eloise's life miserable.

Was this what not sleeping with a woman did to him? He couldn't have her in his bed, so instead he started finding other reasons to be near her? They'd agreed to be friends, but this felt like something...different. Something that could be a whole lot more troublesome.

Tessa would probably rather he just slept with her and got it over with.

But Stefan the director might not. And until that part was in the bag... Eloise was still off limits. And maybe even after that, if what Tessa said was true. Noah could be staring down a long period of acting-enforced celibacy.

Unless... Tessa had only said to be discreet. He hadn't thought that could be possible with Eloise, with the world watching them at Melissa's wedding. But they were *supposed* to be spending time together. Nobody could talk about that. And seeing her fade into the background, realising how much she truly didn't want to be watched... If there was anyone he could have a discreet fling with, despite his celebrity, it would be Eloise.

If he could convince her. Which was by no means a sure thing, given her feelings about actors.

The music came to an end at last, and Melissa hugged him close before stepping away again. 'Right! Eloise's turn.' She turned to her maid of honour, smiling in a way that Noah could only describe as predatory.

She was waiting for Eloise to fail, he realised. If it hadn't been for the world's media watching, Melissa might even have waited until the day to tell Eloise about the dance and let her humiliate herself in front of everyone. But, since she wouldn't risk her perfect wedding that way, this was obviously the next best thing.

No wonder Eloise looked as if she'd rather be anywhere but there.

He moved towards her, reaching out a hand to pull her into his arms.

'I apologise in advance for treading on your feet,' she said, and he smiled.

'You'll be fine. I'm hardly a professional dancer either, you realise? I'm best known for smashing through walls and beating people up.'

'That's true.' She looked rather pleased about that fact, strangely.

'So you *do* know my films.' He grinned, more pleased by the fact that she was looking a little more relaxed at last than by the acknowledgement of his fame.

Eloise rolled her eyes. 'Yes, fine. Everybody knows Noah Cross. You're on, like, every billboard and every bus.'

'Not *all* of them.'

'Most, then. All those big budget blockbusters you're always starring in.' She frowned. 'But you didn't always do those, did you? Didn't I read somewhere that you used to be on the stage?'

This time, Noah *was* surprised. 'Yes, actually. Not many people remember my touring actor days now, though. I did a three-year stint as a stage actor, touring in a company that took Shakespeare all over the States.'

'Huh.' She tilted her head to look at him. 'I suppose I could buy you as Hamlet.'

'Not Romeo?' He waggled his eyebrows in a suggestive manner, and Eloise laughed as the music started up again.

Melissa's voice rang out around the room. 'And dance!'

Of course, he hadn't had time to actually talk Eloise through the steps, since they'd been busy discussing him, but she seemed to have picked up the basics from watching Melissa anyway. 'You're a quick study,' he said as they spun.

'My mum made me take dance lessons when I was younger,' Eloise admitted, still looking down at her feet. 'I did ballet, tap, modern, lyrical and even a couple of terms of ballroom. Apparently I haven't quite forgotten everything.'

'Then why were you nervous?' Noah asked. She'd been terrified at the prospect of dancing; he'd seen it in her face. But why, if she already knew she could do it?

'It's not the dancing,' Eloise admitted. But, before she could tell him exactly what the problem was, Melissa was striding across the floor towards them.

'You're doing it wrong,' the bride said, grabbing Eloise's arm and yanking her away from Noah.

'I thought she had it, actually,' Noah objected,

but Melissa had already taken up her ballroom position.

'No. I'll show you again,' she said to Eloise with exaggerated patience.

Noah raised his arms and met Eloise's gaze over Melissa's shoulder. She raised her eyes to the heavens, and he smiled.

Maybe he'd tread on Melissa's toes while they danced. That might persuade her to give up on the lessons.

Or at least put Eloise back in his arms, which couldn't be a bad thing.

CHAPTER SEVEN

MELISSA DRILLED THEM in their dance for far longer than Eloise thought was strictly necessary—she wasn't *that* bad, she was sure. Eventually, though, Melissa had to let Eloise go, once she pointed out that if she didn't there would be no one to check that everything was ready for the Frost Fair.

Noah took the opportunity to escape too, which Eloise was grateful for. It had felt too good, dancing in his arms. And the connection between them—even if it was born entirely out of mocking Melissa—seemed a little too easy. She wasn't an idiot; she knew Noah was just playing with her. What she didn't understand was why he was still bothering. She'd made her position on the subject of having flings with actors painfully clear the night before.

Maybe that was it—the challenge. She could see Noah as the kind of guy who grew tired of always getting everything he wanted handed to him on a plate. Some people were happy to carry on that way, enjoying the ease that sort of life gave them. But Noah… She got the impression he liked to work for things a little more. Hadn't he said something last night about a new role in a film, something more challenging? Yes, that had to be it. She was a different sort of challenge; that was all. The moment she gave in, all the fun would be gone for him.

She had to remember that.

Dressed again in her navy work dress and chocolate leather boots, Eloise hurried down to the riverbank, her coat wrapped warmly around her. The preparations for the afternoon's Frost Fair were well underway—which was just as well, as Laurel would be bringing the guests down from the hotel within the hour.

Wooden stalls were laid out all along the riverbank, a temporary street of tempting offerings to eat, drink or enjoy. The river that ran beside the hotel rarely froze and, even if it had, it would have been a health and safety impossibility to hold the fair actually *on* the ice, like people would have done at the Frost Fairs of old. But, with the rustic stalls, the lute music drifting through the icy air as the musicians warmed up and the smell of the hog roast cooking, it *almost* felt authentic.

Authentic enough for Hollywood, anyway, Eloise figured.

Pulling out her clipboard, she did the rounds, checking in with every stallholder, every caterer, every entertainer, from jugglers to ice carvers. Everything was looking good until she reached the small stage set up at the far end of the fair, ready for the acting troupe Laurel had hired to entertain the masses with excerpts from Shakespeare's plays.

'How's it going?' she asked a dour-looking man unloading period costumes and props onto a rack.

Hang on. No, he wasn't unloading. He was taking the costumes off the rack and putting them back into the suitcase.

'Not great,' he said, reaching for another doublet. 'The troupe minibus gave up the ghost halfway down the M4. The guy they sent out to fix it said it's dead as a doornail. I'd come on ahead with the costumes and props, but I'm only the stage manager-slash-accompanist. You want period sound effects or music? I'm your man.' He shook his head. 'Not a lot of use without the actors, though. Figured I might as well pack up again.'

'Wait. Don't… Stop packing up. Please. Just stop it.' The man held up his hands and stepped back as Eloise reached for her phone.

'Your call, love, but I don't see what good they'll do you.'

'I just need to make a phone call…' Turning away, Eloise stabbed at her phone until it rang Laurel, holding it tight to her ear and praying that the wedding planner would have an idea.

Click. 'You have reached the voicemail of Laurel Sommers, wedding planner.'

Of course, to be any help at all she'd have to actually pick up the phone. Eloise hung up and tried again.

After she got put through to voicemail for the fifth time, Eloise gave up.

'Okay, look, we'll sort this out,' she said, turning back to the man with the props. Except now he wasn't alone.

'Alas, poor Yorick!' Noah held a skull at arm's length as he quoted the line from *Hamlet*, looking utterly in his element.

Hadn't he said he'd been a Shakespearean actor once? Maybe he could be again…

Spotting her, Noah put down the skull and walked towards her. Eloise pasted on her brightest, most winning smile and hoped he still wanted to keep playing their little game. Because she needed a big favour.

The Frost Fair, Noah had to admit, was quite the set-up. It looked like something from some high fantasy epic movie, rather than a historical. Stallholders were wandering around in that pseudo-period costume that seemed to work for peasants of all eras, mostly in shades of brown and green with the odd berry-red hat for a spot of colour. The river rushed past beside the stalls, flowing over rocks and under bare trees. The spot must be beautiful in the summer, he realised. No wonder Melissa had wanted to come back here.

When he came across the stage, he couldn't resist—especially when he saw the box of props waiting there, just asking to be used. It might be a cliché, but in his experience it was a rare actor who could resist a bit of *Hamlet*.

Then he saw Eloise, lowering her phone from her ear, her red hair the brightest thing in the whole fair. Even her sensible brown knee boots and knitted navy dress made him want to reach out and touch her.

And when she smiled…his heart contracted in his chest.

Then his eyes narrowed. That was not the smile of a woman planning a seduction. That was the smile of a woman who wanted something. Well, he wasn't above giving—as long as he got something in return.

In all honesty, if it was Eloise asking, he'd probably do it for free. Just to see some more of that smile.

'What do you need?' he asked as she approached.

Her smile faltered for a moment, then came back stronger than ever. 'The troupe of actors we'd hired to perform today can't make it. Their minibus broke down about a hundred miles away.'

'That's a shame.' Noah was pretty sure he could guess now what she wanted, but he was going to make her ask, all the same. Given how incapable of saying no to her he felt right now, it was only fair.

'I don't suppose you're feeling in the mood to reprise some of your more famous Shakespearian roles, are you?'

'Fancying some Romeo at last, huh?'

'Or Hamlet, or Benedick, or Puck…I'm not fussed, as long as there's someone up on that stage performing when our guests arrive.'

'Aren't I one of those guests?'

Eloise shook her head. 'You're the best man. That means pitching in and fixing whatever goes wrong with the wedding.'

'I suppose it does,' Noah said slowly, an idea forming in his mind. 'And I guess as maid of honour you have to do the same, right?'

Her eyes widened. 'Well, in principle…but you're the actor here. This really seems like a job for you.'

'Ah, but it would be so much better with two, wouldn't it?' Noah said. 'Monologues are so boring. But a good bit of dialogue…that'll get people watching. So, how's *your* Shakespeare?'

'Rusty. Very, very rusty. I mean, I used to help

my mum learn her lines, and she did a few of Shakespeare's, but that was years ago. As was my A-level English Lit course, for that matter.'

'Your mum?' Noah frowned. 'She was an actress?' Did *that* explain Eloise's strange prejudice against actors? Had one messed her mother around? Or was her dad an actor?

For someone he knew so little about, he felt strangely invested in her past. And in her immediate future, come to that.

'Of a sort. Look, it doesn't matter now. The point is, I don't know the lines. Any lines. For any play.'

'You don't need to,' Noah told her, pushing aside his questions about her parents for a time when Eloise was less stressed. So, some time next year, probably. The woman had been stress incarnate since he'd met her. Strange— that wasn't something he'd ever found attractive before. 'We'll do readings rather than acting out the scenes. It'll work fine and you don't need to worry about remembering anything.'

Eloise frowned. 'I suppose. But…'

Now they were getting to it. 'So, what's the real reason you don't want to do it? Worried I'll show you up? Trust me, I wouldn't. It's a long time since I've done Shakespeare too.'

She pulled a face. 'That's not it. Well, yes, partly, I suppose. You're an actual actor. I'm someone who's just read the plays a few times.'

'I'm an actor who mostly beats people up in films these days,' he reminded her. 'But, actually, I'm looking to get into some different roles, so maybe a change of pace will be good for me. And I think fooling around on stage with me will be good for you too. We can just do the comedies, if you like. It'll be fun.'

'Fun? Standing up there with the famous and the beautiful watching me make a fool of myself? *Not* my idea of a good time.'

'That's what you're worried about? Them?' Noah shook his head. He knew from personal experience that nobody attending this wedding thought too much about anyone except themselves. 'I really wouldn't.'

'Easy for you to say. I don't...' She swallowed and met his gaze. 'I told you. I really don't like being the centre of attention.'

So that was it. 'That's why you didn't want to

do the dance either,' he said, remembering how she'd shrunk away, almost disappearing into the wall, when she'd been watching him and Melissa dance that morning. 'And why you wear such boring clothes.'

'Leave my clothes out of it,' she grumbled. 'Not everyone has to be a peacock like Melissa.'

'Or a show-off like me,' he finished for her. 'But it doesn't matter. That's the joy of acting. *You're* not the centre of attention at all—your character is. You can be someone else for a while. It's fantastically freeing.'

'Really?' Eloise didn't look entirely convinced.

'Sure. Why do you think so many actors are screwed up as human beings? It's not the job that does it. It's the reason they choose the job in the first place. Who else would pick a career that lets them escape from themselves?'

'I suppose,' Eloise allowed. 'But that doesn't change the fact that it *would* be me up there on the stage. Making a fool of myself.'

'I won't let you do that.' He reached out a hand to take hers. 'Come on. It'll be fun. I promise.' It would be, he was certain. And fun was definitely something Eloise needed more of in her life.

She sucked in a deep breath, so deep he could see her chest move. 'Okay,' she said at last. 'Let's do this.'

If women in Shakespeare's time really wore dresses as uncomfortable as the one Noah picked out for her, suddenly Eloise understood why they always looked so miserable in paintings. She'd almost rather be wearing the hideous bridesmaid's dress. Almost.

'Perfect,' Noah said as she stepped out from the Portaloo she'd used as a changing room. Apparently stardom wasn't all it was cracked up to be.

'I feel like an idiot.'

'But you look like a star,' Noah promised.

Eloise glanced down at the corseted bodice, the intricate lacing and embroidery and the full skirt. The deep winter green of the fabric suited her, she knew, and the golden stitching added something special to the dress. But it wasn't until she met Noah's gaze and saw the warmth and approval in his eyes that she truly believed she looked okay.

More than okay, if the way Noah's gaze travelled her body was anything to go by. She almost wished there was a full-length mirror around so she could see for herself.

But she knew that the prettiest costume couldn't hide her from the reality of what she was about to do.

Why had she agreed to this? How had she let him convince her? He hadn't even really had to try—he'd just smiled at her and told her it would be fun, and she'd fallen for it.

This was why she needed to stay away from Noah Cross. Something that would be a lot easier if they weren't both in the wedding party from hell.

'Are you ready?' Noah asked as they stood at the side of the stage.

'No.'

Noah smiled, and handed her the first reading they'd decided on—one of her favourite exchanges between Beatrice and Benedick from *Much Ado About Nothing*.

'You can do this,' he whispered. Then he took her hand and led her out onto the stage.

It had been so many years since she'd done this, Eloise had thought she must have forgotten how. But as she stood there, script in shaking hand, it all came flooding back. The tiny local theatre in her home town, just a few miles away from where she stood now. The scruffy red velvet seats in the audience. The way the wood of the stage smelt. The heavy curtains that rose and fell on their shows.

Eloise, twelve years old, standing in the chorus line of their latest musical, watching her mother fall in love with her leading man, rehearsal after rehearsal. And her father in the wings, humiliated again. And knowing, even then, that this affair wouldn't last either. That everyone would talk—in whispers, if her dad was around, and openly if he wasn't—and predict when they might make it official. Whether this time Letitia would leave, find a man who could be equal to her instead of staying with her boring, grey old husband.

And every time she would threaten to walk out, there'd be scenes—on stage and off. And every time, as the last night ended, Eloise would know it would all be over soon. That her mother would never really leave, never really chase the perfect happiness and true love she claimed she wanted.

Because if she was happy, where would the drama be? Letitia lived for the drama, not the love.

She'd even chosen drama over her own daughter when she'd seduced Derek away from her. Eloise was under no illusions about what mattered most to her mother—or to actors in general.

Noah gave her a look and she took a breath, smiled and began the act. She'd taken all the drama classes, played her parts in the society beside her parents, so she knew what she was doing.

But she would never be an actress. Not when she'd already seen how much happiness it could destroy.

It was easy to lose herself in the lines, the humour, the characters. Noah had been right about that, at least. Up there on the stage, she could almost believe she was another person and that made it a lot easier.

They hadn't planned a full performance, as such, so there was no start time and no audience waiting patiently for them to start. Instead, they began the scene as the guests started to mill around the Frost Fair, and waited to be discovered. By the time Eloise looked out from the stage after the third scene she and Noah had chosen, she was amazed to find that they had drawn quite a crowd.

As they applauded, Noah took the script from her and gave her the next one. Eloise frowned as she looked at the highlighted passage. This wasn't one she'd agreed to. They'd said comedies only, and *Romeo and Juliet* was most certainly *not* a comedy.

'Ready?' Noah whispered and, before she could answer, said his opening line.

It was the scene at the masked ball, Eloise realised as she responded. That short, incredibly flirtatious and sexy scene where they dance and talk and...

'Then move not while my prayer's effect I take.'

She barely had a moment to register Noah's words before his hands were at her waist, tugging her close. He kissed her lightly, just a brief press of his lips against hers. But it was enough. Enough to send sparks through her whole body, to leave her aching and desperate for more.

Wait. He'd just said something. Which meant she had another line.

Somewhere, from the recesses of her memory and an abiding love for the movie version, she found it.

'Then have my lips the sin that they have took.'

Noah grinned, still holding her against him.

'Sin from my lips?' he said. *'O trespass sweetly urged. Give me my sin again.'*

Again? Eloise's eyes widened but he just kept smiling at her—before dipping her deeply over his arm and lowering his lips to hers.

There was nothing brief about this kiss. Nothing perfunctory. And nothing about it felt like an act.

Her hands tightened on the fabric of Noah's doublet as he deepened the kiss, teasing her mouth open and driving her wild. Her whole body reacted to the sensation of his lips on hers, tightening and tensing with the need to take things further. If they hadn't been in public...

A whoop went up from the crowd and reality came crashing in on her. They weren't just in public. She was on a stage, in front of the Hollywood elite, some of her staff and probably her teenage nemesis. Making out with a famous actor like some girl with a crush.

She tried to pull away but, since Noah was the only thing holding her up, she didn't get too far. Fortunately, he seemed to sense the change of mood and slowly raised her back to a standing position, only ending the kiss at the last possible moment.

The audience cheered, clapping and whistling, and Eloise knew her face had to be the same colour as her hair.

'Okay?' Noah whispered, too soft to be heard over the crowd.

But Eloise couldn't answer. The only words she could find were Juliet's.

'*You kiss by the book,*' she declared, and the crowd laughed.

She was glad someone found it funny. Because, as far as Eloise was concerned, that kiss meant only one thing.

She was in big trouble.

'*You kiss by the book.*'

Eloise sounded suitably stunned, but the way she projected the line into the crowd left Noah uncertain. Was she still acting? Or had the kiss affected her the same way it had him?

Because he definitely hadn't been acting.

Oh, the first kiss, sure. That had just been a joke, almost. He'd slipped the short *Romeo and Juliet* exchange in while Eloise had been getting changed, partly because it was one of his favourites and partly because it gave him an excuse to kiss her. He'd purposefully kept that first kiss light and relaxed, giving her the freedom to pull back any time she liked, even if it *was* only an act.

But from the moment his lips had met hers he'd known that wouldn't be enough. The electricity between them, the way her touch sparked through his body, heating him to boiling point even in the freezing English air...that *couldn't* all be pretend, could it? And then, of course, he'd had to know for sure.

So he'd kissed her. Properly.

And his whole world had tilted.

The audience were applauding again, and Noah realised he'd almost forgotten they were there. He hadn't been playing to the crowd for once, or thinking about how his moves would look on the big screen. The only thing that had been on his mind was the woman in his arms.

Never mind Tessa and her admonitions to behave. Never mind his reputation. Even the role of Marcus hadn't mattered for the long moments where he'd held Eloise.

He blinked and the spell was broken, and the real world surged back in.

Her final line spoken, Eloise tried to make a dash for the edge of the makeshift stage but he grabbed her hand to keep her with him, his mind churning. When she glared at him, he explained softly, 'We have to take a bow.'

Her glare didn't lessen, but she gave a sharp nod and took her place beside him. Hand in hand, they bowed to the assembled audience, who whooped and cheered even louder.

'What were they serving at those drinks stands?' Noah asked. Because he was good, he knew that, and Eloise had been fabulous, but this level of enthusiasm still seemed a little over the top. Unless they'd seen the truth behind the kiss—but he doubted that too. This crowd wouldn't know truth if it kissed them.

'Spiced apple cider.' Eloise didn't look at him as she answered, smiling out at the crowd as they took their second bow.

'Alcoholic.'

'Apparently very.'

'Encore!' someone in the crowd yelled but Eloise shook her head and, before Noah could stop her, she was across the stage and descending the steps, ready to disappear back into the mass of people filling the Frost Fair. Suddenly Noah was alone on the stage, wondering if her reaction to the kiss meant she was more or less likely to let him do it again.

Because one thing he was very sure of. He wanted to kiss Eloise Miller in a way he hadn't wanted to kiss anyone for years.

In fact, he wanted to do a lot more than kiss her. Discreetly, of course. But that kiss had proved that Eloise was worth taking the risk.

And, after the way she'd responded to him, she was going to have to come up with a better excuse than *I don't date actors* to convince him that she didn't want exactly the same thing.

CHAPTER EIGHT

ELOISE REFUSED TO dwell on the memory of Noah's kiss, instead throwing herself into traipsing around the Frost Fair to make sure that everything was going perfectly. Then, when the stallholders started looking irritated at her interference and Laurel assured her that she had everything in hand, Eloise stormed off back to the hotel to get out of her ridiculous costume and into something more appropriate for Melissa's hen night.

By the time the bride, bridesmaids and other favoured female guests were gathered for games, pink drinks and the wearing of feather boas in the main bar that evening, Eloise could still feel the memory of Noah's lips against hers.

How was she supposed to think about anything else after a kiss like that? She'd barely managed to focus on her job long enough to check everything was in place for the hen night. And choosing a dress... Well, what did one wear after wearing Juliet's best frock all afternoon? Eloise's wardrobe certainly had nothing so fancy. In the end, she'd settled on another navy dress—one of four in her wardrobe. This one, at least, was made of more slippery material than her thick, knitted work one, and it skimmed over her body in a way that suggested that she might actually have some curves under the fabric. Somewhere.

Just in case Noah felt the sudden need to reprise their roles of Romeo and Juliet, she told herself. After all, if it was *Juliet* kissing Noah rather than Eloise, that couldn't be so bad, right?

No. That was crazy. And that was *exactly* the sort of thinking that had seen her mother fall into affair after affair with her leading men.

Eloise had sworn her whole life that she wouldn't make the same mistakes. That she wouldn't get caught up in the spectacle of a love affair and miss the reality underneath. She'd rather a boring, predictable romance to the high drama of the ones her mother had enjoyed anyway. And she wouldn't let movie star good looks and charm sway her from that.

No matter how incredible his kisses were.

They'd said friends. That was what she had to stick to. That was what she needed to get her through this nightmare of a wedding—a friend.

'Of course, Eloise had *loads* of practice at being on stage, didn't you?' Melissa waved her champagne flute across the table in Eloise's direction as she spoke, and Eloise scrambled to try and catch up on the conversation she'd been ignoring in favour of reliving Noah's kiss.

'Sorry?'

Melissa rolled her eyes. 'The girls were just talking about your performance at the Frost Fair this afternoon.'

'You were fantastic!' one of the guests Eloise had met only briefly, and didn't recognise from the movies at all, said. She had a feeling the woman was the wife of a director or something similar. 'You really brought the whole Frost Fair to life.'

Eloise looked down at her hands to try and hide her blush.

'And I was saying how you'd had lots of practice on the stage,' Melissa went on. 'Totally different to the movies, of course. But all those years taking part in those local plays with your mum was obviously good for something, wasn't it?'

Melissa's gaze met hers as she spoke, and Eloise felt the threat in her words as she mentioned her mother. A chill ran through her at the calculating look in Melissa's eyes. The unspoken message was clear: upstage the bride again, and everyone would get to hear about Eloise's mother's antics.

Everything Eloise had spent the last ten years living down would be public knowledge all over again.

'Perhaps it's time for the first game?' Eloise stood and clapped her hands together, deflecting the conversation away from herself.

Melissa, mollified for the time being, beamed as her guests threw themselves into games that thrust her back into the centre of attention. Eloise, meanwhile, found herself watching from the sidelines, noting every other instance of Melissa manipulating the evening to keep herself on top. Like the way the bridesmaids were all just slightly less beautiful and famous than she was. Or how guests with little to give in a professional sense were kept on the outskirts of the gathering, while much attention was given to those in power—directors, actresses with more Hollywood pull. The tiered system Melissa had in place was obvious, now she knew what she was looking for.

Clearly Melissa had managed to keep her reputation for sweetness intact in the film industry, the same way she always had when working at Morwen Hall. But Eloise was sure there must be people in Hollywood who had experienced the other side of Melissa too—as she had all those years ago.

She couldn't help but wonder what would happen if one of those people suddenly became more famous and powerful than Melissa.

'Time for Balloon Question Time!' Laurel, official hen party planner, clapped her hands and distracted the group from laughing at the male body parts they'd all been making out of modelling clay for the previous game. Eloise, having observed their efforts, was glad of the change of pace.

'Now, this game has a bit of a twist,' Laurel said, looking at Eloise with an apology in her eyes as she spoke. 'We have twenty questions in these twenty balloons in the net. The pink balloons hold questions for the bride. The purple balloons have questions for the bridesmaids and maid of honour to answer.'

Eloise groaned, hoping the sound was covered by the excited chatter of the other hens and the music playing in the bar. Just what she needed—more attention.

'So, ladies, line up and prepare to pop balloons! Bride, bridesmaids and maid of honour, come on down!' Melissa, Iona and Caitlin followed Laurel's instructions and took their seats on the barstools lined up on the platform by the bar. Eloise followed more slowly.

'Want to give me a heads up?' she whispered to Laurel as she passed.

'Sorry, no can do. I didn't set the questions. Melissa did.' Laurel patted her on the arm. 'On the plus side, if you refuse to answer any of them, you get to drink a shot.'

More alcohol. That would help.

The first few balloons went well. Each guest took a turn popping one, then reading out the question inside, directing it at the bride or attendants depending on its colour. Melissa answered questions about her first boyfriend—where she shot a warning look at Eloise before lying through her teeth—and the role she'd most like to play on film, Marie Antoinette, which Eloise could totally see. Caitlin answered the question about her biggest regret, and Iona one about her favourite memory of Melissa.

And then, with the next purple balloon, it was Eloise's turn.

'Well, this seems very appropriate today,' Laurel said, grinning. Eloise felt something inside her relax. Laurel obviously felt that this was a safe question. How bad could it be? 'Eloise, tell us— in detail—about your best ever kiss.'

The room burst into laughter—all except Melissa, who sat stony-faced beside her. She must have written the questions before the Frost Fair, Eloise realised. Laurel had been setting up the games while the festivities were still going on, so she must have had the questions beforehand. There was no way Melissa wanted to draw attention back to Eloise and Noah's kiss.

'I think we all *saw* the answer to that this afternoon!' Caitlin said, and took another sip from her bright pink cocktail. 'So, tell us! How did it feel?'

Melissa snorted—which led Eloise to assume she'd had one too many cocktails. 'As if we don't all already know that? Noah Cross must have dated almost every woman in this room.'

'I went to an awards ceremony with him,' Iona said. 'But he never kissed *me* like that.'

'Or me,' someone else piped up.

'He didn't kiss me at all,' another woman added. Eloise frowned. She might think that Noah's playboy reputation was a lie, except anyone who kissed like he did had clearly been practising a *lot*.

'It was just a kiss,' Eloise said, realising that the hens were still waiting for an answer. 'It wasn't even a real one. We were acting.'

'Looked pretty real to me,' Caitlin said.

'That is sort of the idea, Cait,' Melissa snapped. 'Although I appreciate you might not have reached that lesson in your drama training yet.'

There was a moment of stunned silence, and Melissa obviously realised she'd stepped out of her perfect friend character. She turned to Eloise and beamed. 'It did look very real though, I suppose. But then, that shouldn't be such a surprise, should it? It must be in the genes.'

Iona frowned. 'In the jeans? They were in period costume.'

'Genes with a G,' Melissa said sharply. 'Eloise's mother was an actress too, you see, locally,
anyway. And she was absolutely famous for her
ability to make all her leading men fall in love
with her. Wasn't she?'

Eloise froze, the shame and humiliation crest-
ing over her like a wave, just at the reminder.
Melissa knew every single story that had ever
been told about Eloise's mother. Her own mother
had been the one spreading the rumours, most
of the time.

She tried to tell herself that it didn't matter—
that these people, flown in for the week for a
wedding, would be out of her life in just a few
days. They didn't care about her, didn't care about
her past. They had no importance in her life.

But knowing that didn't make any difference.
The humiliation she'd endured at the hands of
her mother's behaviour for so many years hadn't
faded, even now. She wouldn't ever shake those
painful memories, she knew. The whispers, the
whole town talking about her, casting sympa-
thetic—or worse, mocking—glances at her fa-

ther. Everyone she knew expecting her to turn out the exact same way.

'She sounds like quite the lady,' Caitlin said, eyeing Eloise with more interest than she'd ever shown previously. 'Did she ever try to make it professionally?'

'She used to be a dancer in London, didn't she, Eloise?' Melissa asked lightly. 'You know the sort.'

'Sure.' Iona laughed. 'Well, everyone has to start somewhere.'

'And those without the talent stay there,' Caitlin finished, sending a ripple of amusement through the crowd.

'It was sad, really,' Melissa said. 'She must have been quite beautiful once, I suppose. But you know how older women get sometimes, when they're worried about being left on the shelf, or can't find satisfaction in their marriage. They start running after everything that moves, no matter how ridiculous they look. She even went after your own boyfriend once, didn't she, Eloise? And got him too, as I recall.' She shook her head. 'Poor woman; she clearly had issues.' As if that false sympathy, tacked on the end, somehow made up for the fact that she was trashing

Eloise's mother's name—and Eloise's reputation at the same time.

'Does Noah know about your family tendency to seduce co-stars?' Melissa turned her most innocent smile and wide eyes on Eloise.

Eloise couldn't take it any more. 'Melissa, could I please have a word with you outside?' she ground out between clenched teeth.

'But darling! We're all having so much fun here!'

'I just remembered something about the arrangements for the…ah…photo shoot tomorrow. I'd hate for anything to go wrong.'

Melissa rolled her eyes and slid off her barstool. 'Oh, fine. Honestly, finding capable people these days… You guys all carry on having fun! I'll be right back.'

Eloise stalked out of the bar into the empty corridor, breathing deeply in the hope that she'd be able to talk to Melissa rationally and calmly. Like a grown-up. Like she'd never managed to do with her before.

'So, what's the problem?' Melissa asked, all trace of her affected friendliness gone.

'I'd rather you didn't bring my mother into conversations, please,' Eloise said as calmly as possible. 'My family history has no bearing on this wedding, and I'm sure your friends don't care about who my mother slept with over a decade ago.'

'I'm sure they don't either,' Melissa said, her tone sharp. 'Your mother was a slut and a disgrace, but who cares about that now, right? But if *you're* sleeping with Noah Cross, you can bet everyone in Hollywood will care about that. It'll be the biggest story of my wedding—and that is unacceptable.'

'I'm not...I'm not sleeping with Noah. I only just met the guy,' Eloise said, taken aback.

'So? What difference does that make?' Melissa asked. 'He's a huge name, he's gorgeous, he's loaded and he's interested. Of course you're going to sleep with him. You'd be an idiot not to. But *not* at my wedding, okay?'

Melissa turned and strode back into the bar, her perfect smile in place on her perfect face. Eloise stared after her, stunned.

'But... But I'm not sleeping with Noah Cross,' she said again, to the empty hallway.

'And isn't that a crying shame?' Noah said from behind her.

* * *

Noah hadn't meant to gatecrash the hen night. It was just that he felt about ten years too old for the stag do. Not in actual age, he supposed, but in maturity. And, given that he regularly expected to be the least mature guy at the table, that was saying something.

Riley might be getting married, but he still seemed like a kid to Noah. It was as if the whole wedding was a game, another act. That at the end of the day he could take his ring off and go back to being just Riley again—no harm, no foul.

Marriage meant somewhat more to Noah. That was why he had no intention of ever entertaining the institution.

Still, even knowing that not everyone in Hollywood shared his opinion on the importance of marriage, he hadn't expected the stag do to feel so…shallow. Meaningless.

Irrationally, he blamed Eloise. She was the opposite of shallow. She'd given him false expectations for the rest of the world.

He hadn't even been looking for Eloise, particularly. He'd been looking for a drink—a proper one, not a cup from the keg Riley had insisted on, as a homage to frat movies past. But when he'd heard Eloise's voice…he had to admit that maybe it had been her he'd been looking for all along.

Melissa spat out something hateful about Eloise's mother, and Eloise responded with a denial. Noah moved in closer, in time to hear Melissa rate all the things about him that mattered in her world, none of which were anything he'd want to feature in his obituary.

Then she left, and Eloise was alone in the hallway.

'I'm not sleeping with Noah Cross,' she said.

Noah stepped out of the shadows. 'And isn't that a crying shame?'

Eloise spun round, her eyes wide. 'What are you doing here?'

'Just looking for a drink.' Was it the lights, or was that something akin to lust that he saw in her eyes? 'And you.'

'Why?'

He didn't have an answer. It should have been easy—*I want you. I desire you.* He'd been sure that was all this was, this strange attraction between them. A game, a flirtation. A friendship with edge, that was all. At least until the kiss they'd shared at the Frost Fair.

Now…now he had no idea what this was, or why the need to be with her was thrumming through his body like a second heartbeat.

But it was. And he did need her. Right now.

Discretion be damned.

Noah moved forward, closing the distance between them in just a couple of steps. Eloise licked her lips, just a quick brush of her pink tongue against her lower lip, but it was enough to drive Noah wild. Enough for him to imagine those lips on his own again. To imagine them on his skin, covering his body, while his own mouth touched every single inch of her…

No, he had no idea what this was between them. But he knew he was done fighting it.

He wrapped his arms around her waist, just as he had on the stage that afternoon. But this time there were no costumes, no parts. No Romeo, no Juliet. Just Noah and Eloise.

She stared up at him, her lips parted, her pupils so large they almost eclipsed the blue-green of her beautiful eyes. She wanted this as badly as he did; he could see it.

But the most frightening thing was, he wasn't sure that a kiss would be enough. Or one night. Or several nights.

He wanted her body, sure, but what scared him was how much *more* he wanted. What was it about Eloise that made him want to look deeper? To know more, to understand?

Deeper was off the table—and had been since Sally.

But if it hadn't been…he had a feeling that Eloise was a woman he could have shown every inch of his soul, and come to know hers in return.

He shook his head, just an inch or so, just enough to dismiss the thoughts. He'd known the woman a couple of days. That wasn't what this was about, for either of them.

All he needed to concentrate on was kissing her again.

He didn't say anything—words were unnecessary now. As he stared into Eloise's eyes he knew she understood everything he wasn't saying. He tilted his head, lowering his lips to hers, and she rose up on her toes to meet him, pressing her body against his. He could feel every inch of her pressed against him, warm and soft and wanting where they touched, and he couldn't help but deepen the kiss. It took everything he had not to sweep her up against the nearest wall and make love to her, without a thought for who might see or what they'd think. Or what might get back to Stefan, the director, who needed to believe that Noah could control his baser instincts.

Usually, he could, Noah was sure. He remembered having control, willpower, restraint once. Before he'd met Eloise.

He'd never felt this before—this desperate, unthinking desire. He'd dated the world's most beautiful women and he'd had true love, yet none of them had ever inspired this sort of passion down deep inside of him.

Noah didn't want to think too much about what that meant. He just wanted to enjoy it.

But then Eloise pulled away.

Noah let his hands fall from her waist as she stepped back, staring up at him, her mouth half open as if she wanted to talk but couldn't quite get the words out. After a moment of wordless staring, she swallowed and said, 'Not here. Please, not here.'

'Right. Of course.' This was a bad idea. This

was everything he'd sworn he wouldn't do this week. 'I should go.'

But then Eloise met his gaze and shook her head before she turned away, stalking up the hallway towards the stairs.

He watched her go, his whole body at war with his mind. His feet ached to follow her, his arms to reach out and grab her. But his mind told him to stop this now, before it grew too much. Too dangerous.

Never mind that it could jeopardise the first movie role he'd been excited about in seven years. As much as he wanted it right now, the film seemed like the least important thing in his world.

There was a reason he didn't normally feel this way about women—he didn't let himself. But Eloise had pierced through every defence he'd ever built in less than forty-eight hours. How much more damage could she do with another day?

His eyes fell shut as he willed his body to leave it be.

But this time his body won out.

It took seconds to catch her up, halfway up the stairs to the third floor, but she didn't acknowledge his presence at all. Which at least meant she wasn't sending him away. In silence, they made their way up the stairs, down darkened hallways, to a room at the far corner of the hotel.

Eloise's hands shook as she reached for her key, and he leaned over to take it from her without thinking. She rested against the door, her back to the wood as she looked up at him, her eyes vulnerable now. Wary.

'I said I wouldn't do this,' she whispered. So had he. But some things couldn't be denied.

'Because you don't want to?' he asked softly. 'Or because Melissa told you not to?'

'Because I'm not normally this person.'

'Do you want to be?'

If she said no, he'd walk away. The frustration might kill him but he'd do it. But he didn't think she would. He'd seen something deeper in her—something more than she'd admit to. She might try and hide herself in those dark and dull dresses, might pin her beautiful hair back so it didn't blaze so brightly, but she couldn't hide who she really was for ever.

And Noah had a feeling that the real Eloise Miller would be spectacular.

How could he not want to see her in all her glory?

'If you ask me to go,' he said, his voice hoarse, 'I'll go.'

She bit her lip, then reached out to take the key from him again.

'Don't go,' she whispered, and Noah's whole soul sang.

CHAPTER NINE

WHAT WAS SHE DOING? What on *earth* was she doing?

Well, Eloise thought as Noah kissed her deeply, pressing her up against the wood of her bedroom door, whatever she was doing felt *fantastic*.

But then reality caught up with her.

'Nobody knows,' she managed to get out between kisses.

Noah tilted his head back from hers and she missed his lips the instant they were gone. 'What?' he asked, sounding hazy with lust.

Good. She shouldn't be the only one losing her mind over this strange attraction between them.

'Nobody knows,' she repeated. 'This is our secret, okay?'

He nodded. 'Fine. Great. Anything. Just open the door.'

The man had a point, Eloise conceded as she turned within the circle of his arms and struggled to open the door with shaking hands. If they didn't get to a bed soon it was very possible they'd both be naked in the corridor within five minutes. Maybe less.

Finally, the door gave way and they tumbled into Eloise's room. It wasn't anywhere near as grand as Noah's, but she didn't imagine he cared very much right then. She definitely didn't.

As she fell onto the bed, Noah's body covering hers, Eloise's last coherent thought before giving in to pleasure was, *As long as it's a secret, no one can get hurt.*

Later, much later, Noah drew lazy patterns on her skin with his clever fingers, and Eloise couldn't even find the energy to care that she was naked beside one of the world's official top ten most beautiful men, and he was staring at her. Her. Boring, embarrassed and blushing Eloise Miller, with her too bright hair and her too tall and straight body.

'You're really good at that,' she managed eventually, the first words either of them had spoken since they'd fallen apart in each other's arms after what seemed like hours of pleasure. In reality…

Eloise squinted at the clock. How had it only been forty-five minutes since she'd been telling Melissa she wasn't sleeping with Noah Cross? 'Practice, I suppose.'

'Maybe I was just very, very motivated.' Noah pressed a kiss to her bare shoulder, then carried on up her neck. Eloise squirmed until he captured her lips and she let herself sink into the kiss.

It was secret. He'd promised. It was just them, just one night.

She could let herself have this, and enjoy it. Just this once.

Noah raised himself up on one elbow so he was looking down at her. Eloise wondered where he'd found the energy. Blinking and breathing were taking all of hers.

'What Melissa was saying before...' Noah trailed off, and Eloise would have groaned if she had the strength. The last thing she wanted to talk about while in bed with Noah Cross was Melissa. 'About your mother...' Noah began again, and she realised she was wrong.

The absolute last thing she *ever* wanted to talk about was her mother.

'It doesn't matter,' she said quickly, hoping she

could end the conversation before it really got started. 'It was a long time ago.'

'It seemed to matter to you earlier. I mean, you promised Melissa you wouldn't sleep with me because of it.'

'And look how well that turned out.'

Noah's smile took on a hint of smugness. 'Chemistry like ours...you can't promise that away. Trust me, I tried.'

'You tried?' If the last couple of days had been Noah trying *not* to sleep with her, he sucked at it.

'Not very hard,' he admitted. 'But you're not the only one who needs to keep this a secret. There's this director... Anyway, it doesn't matter. Let's just say it's not in my best interests to have this be public knowledge either.'

That was good, Eloise thought. If they both needed it to stay secret, they'd both be more motivated to keep it that way. And that meant there was a chance she might survive this week after all.

'So why did you risk it?' she asked, frowning. She wasn't the sort of woman men took risks over. That was definitely her mother, or Melissa. Not her.

'Because I couldn't not,' Noah said, smiling. 'I know my limits when it comes to resisting beautiful women.'

'You've experienced this a lot?' Eloise didn't like that idea. For her, this was a completely new feeling. The idea that Noah had this with every woman he met… It wasn't that she thought she was anything special, exactly. But if she only got one night with him, she at least wanted it to be one he'd remember.

'Never,' Noah swore, his gaze fixed on hers, truth in his eyes. 'Not like this.'

'Me neither,' Eloise whispered. And, worst of all, she was very afraid she might never feel it again. She'd gone twenty-six years without ever feeling anything close, so it didn't seem likely that the kind of intense passion she had with Noah was waiting for her around every corner.

'I don't do this,' Noah admitted, and Eloise raised her eyebrows. He obviously sensed her scepticism because he went on, 'Not the sex. Yes, I've slept with women. Probably less than you think, but that's not the point. I mean…' He sucked in a deep breath. 'Normally, this is easy. Casual. I don't feel the need to ask questions, to get to know a woman's personal history. But with you…it's different. *You're* different.'

Something in Eloise's chest tightened. Part of her wanted to be pleased, to be proud to be something more than the usual casual encounter that Noah indulged in. But another, larger part of her heart was curling up in the corner of her ribcage, wishing he'd move on and stop noticing her.

Because, whatever he said, she knew the truth. He might not feel it now, but Noah Cross didn't do deep and meaningful. Maybe he wanted to hear all about her childhood woes, but would he give her anything in return? She doubted it.

But still she found herself saying, 'What do you want to know?'

'She was an actress, right? Your mother?' Eloise nodded. 'So, is she the reason you don't date actors?'

'I don't date actors because I've known too many of them,' Eloise said with a sigh. 'And most of them were sleeping with my mum.'

Noah winced. 'Ah.'

'Yeah.' She turned onto her side so they were face to face in the darkness, what little light there was coming through the window glinting in his beautiful eyes. 'She was a big fish in a small pond, I guess. She'd been on the West End stage before she had me. She was pregnant when she met my dad.'

'He's not your biological father?'

Eloise shook her head. 'No. But he was the one who was there for me, every moment. Every step of the way.'

'So, what happened? They got married?'

'They did. And they moved out here, back to the town where my dad had grown up. His family were all gone but...he loved this place, and he wanted Mum to love it too. But she didn't.'

Eloise sucked in a deep breath, preparing herself for the rest of the story. Living it had been horrendous, but surely just telling it couldn't be that bad.

She'd never had to tell it before. Everyone else around here just knew.

'The one thing she did like was the Theatre Society. Our town has a small community theatre. A proper stage, raked seats—the whole thing. So, after I was born, Mum joined the Theatre Society. And because she had the experience on the London stage, well, she became the main at-

traction pretty quickly, I think. As long as I remember, she had every starring role in every play
or show they did there. And if she didn't...well,
she'd threaten to walk out until they changed
their minds. They couldn't afford to upset her,
you see. She was their star.'

'I've known actresses like that,' Noah said
drily. 'And actors too. They're not fun to work
with.'

'No. I can't imagine Mum was, for most of the
people in the society. But her leading men...' This
was the hardest part. 'Every production, it was
the same story. They'd cast the best-looking guy
against her, and every time Mum would make
him fall for her. Whether she fell for them too,
I don't know. She always claimed to be desperately in love with them—at least until the show
was over. Then she'd drop them and come back to
Dad, until the next show. But by then...she'd destroyed those men's lives. Their marriages were
in tatters, their reputations ruined. Some had left
their families, lost their friends, sometimes even
their jobs, for Mum. And she just forgot them the
minute the curtain came down.'

'How many times did she do this?' Noah asked, his voice soft.

'Too many. I don't know. Maybe six, or seven? It didn't start until I was about ten, I don't think—or, if it did, she was more discreet about it. But by the time I was a teenager, everyone knew what she was. What she did. And every guy swore she wouldn't get him—but she always did. If she wanted a man, she had him. And every time my dad was left humiliated.'

'But he always took her back. Why?'

'He loved her.' It was as simple and as awful as that. 'And she loved him too, I think. In her way. She always came home in the end, full of apologies and talk about how things would be different. And they were, for a time. It just never lasted.'

Eloise had always known, from watching her parents, that love was as much a trap as a blessing. That she had to be careful who she fell in love with—because that would be the rest of her life, right there. She could leave, or he could, but it wouldn't change the fact that she loved him, and she'd carry that with her every day.

Was it any wonder she'd never let herself feel that deeply before?

And she wasn't going to start with Noah Cross.

'And Melissa held your parents' behaviour over you?' Noah guessed.

'For years. She made sure everyone knew—and told everyone who'd listen that I was just like my mother. So no girls would be friends with me in case I stole their boyfriends, and no guys would risk being seen with me in case people made fun of them. I didn't even have a proper boyfriend until just before I went away to university. There were a couple of guys at school…but Melissa stole them away pretty fast. Then Derek…'

'Derek?' Noah prodded when she trailed off, and Eloise sighed. This was the most humiliating bit.

'The summer before I left for uni, I was in a play at the Theatre Society. I'd been in loads before, but always in the chorus or helping backstage. This was my first real role. And Derek… he was the director. Older than me—he was twenty-five, I think, to my eighteen. But he took a shine to me. He was my first real everything, I suppose.'

Noah shifted closer, something Eloise hadn't thought was possible until she felt his arms holding her tighter. 'What happened?'

'Mum had the lead role, of course. But her leading man broke his leg a couple of weeks into rehearsals. Derek stepped in...'

Noah winced. 'And your mother?'

'Did what she always did.' Eloise shrugged. 'I don't know why I thought it would be any different, just because he was my boyfriend instead of someone else's husband.'

'How did you find out?'

'Melissa, of course. She sent me down to the prop room to fetch something when she knew they were there together.' Eloise swallowed at the memory, her throat suddenly tight. If she thought about it too long, she became eighteen again—in the grip of infatuation, sexual awakening and too many hormones, and seeing all her dreams and illusions shattered in one instant, as she saw her mother half naked against the prop table, and Derek kissing her.

Noah cursed. 'What did you do?'

'I shut the door, walked away and pretended I'd never been there. I finished with Derek, of course, who didn't seem all that disappointed. And then I ran away to university.' She'd been searching for freedom, the ability to be herself, without the baggage of her family history. But all she'd found was that she was the same shy, scared and gullible little girl in a different town.

'And after college you moved back here?' Noah sounded surprised. 'You even came and worked at the same hotel. Why?'

'It was my home,' Eloise said firmly. 'I couldn't let them take that from me. When I first took the chambermaid job here at sixteen, I guess I was just looking for some freedom. But when I came back...it was a safe place. My place.'

'I guess I can understand that,' Noah said, but his tone said he couldn't.

She sighed. 'Also...university wasn't the fresh new life I was hoping for. Turns out I was the same naive and gullible Eloise there too.'

She'd thrown herself into her business studies and, in her final year, a relationship with another student. Everything seemed perfect—they'd talked about setting up an events business together, about heading out into the real world and making it big. Everything she'd dreamed of seemed close to coming true—running her own business, living her own life, making a success of things at last. Until he'd run off with her best ideas and the only friend she'd made at university, leaving all her classmates talking about it.

Really, was it any wonder she avoided love these days?

'Do you want to tell me?' Noah asked, and Eloise shook her head.

'Let's just say, at least the guy who screwed me over personally *and* professionally at uni wasn't an actor.'

Noah didn't press for the whole sordid story, which she appreciated. She'd shared enough of her past disasters for one night.

Instead, he kissed her shoulder and asked, 'Where are your parents now?'

'My dad died while I was at university. My mum…she's still in town. Her memory is going, though. Early onset dementia, the doctors said. She can't even remember everything she did back then. These days she's just a harmless old lady, I suppose. And the town… Well, they haven't forgotten, I don't suppose. But there are newer and better scandals to talk about most of the time.'

'Until Melissa came back and brought it all up again.'

'Yeah.'

Noah sighed. 'Well, I guess that explains a lot about your attitude to actors.'

With a laugh, Eloise lay back, breaking the intense connection between them. She felt lighter, somehow, for telling him everything.

'Of course, you're still hugely biased against us.' Noah followed her, his body pressing against hers as he kissed her again. 'Not all actors are the same, you know.'

'Maybe not,' Eloise allowed. 'But a lot of them are. Look at you—a different girl on your arm in every photo.'

'That's different.'

'How?'

'That's…it's not me,' Noah said. 'It's the Noah Cross the press and the public want to see.'

'So it's all an act. But do the women you take out know that?'

'Always.' Noah's eyes were serious above her. 'I'm always upfront. It's one night, or several, but it's never serious. They know the deal. I never fall for them, never tell them I love them, never give them any expectations.'

'So you try never to hurt anyone.' But was he protecting them or himself? Eloise couldn't be sure. 'Isn't that kind of lonely?'

'Sometimes.'

'So why do it?'

Noah didn't answer. Instead, he rolled over to lie beside her again.

'What about your family?' Eloise asked instead. 'You've heard all about mine. Tell me about yours. Are they proud of you?'

Noah barked out a harsh laugh. 'Not exactly. My dad's opinion of actors is about as good as yours. He thinks we're all entitled, self-obsessed, narcissistic idiots. Not that he'd put it in those words.'

'Why?' Eloise asked. 'I mean, why does he think that? And what about your mother?'

'I grew up in standard middle America. My family were God-fearing, humble and happy to stay at exactly the same level they'd always been. Working a factory job, drinking beer on a Friday night and never looking for anything different.'

'But you weren't,' Eloise guessed.

'No. My best friend and I…we always talked about getting out of town, escaping to LA and seeking fame and fortune.' Noah gave a half smile at the memory. 'I always thought it was a bit of a pipe dream—until the day she said, "Let's go".'

'And you went.'

'Yeah. I did.' He smiled at her. 'And the rest is history.' Leaning in, he pressed kisses over her shoulder, obviously hoping to distract her. But Eloise had more questions.

'Why did you want to know about my mother?' she asked. 'And don't say it's because I'm different. Everybody is different. If you want to know me… I need to know. Why?'

Noah shifted beside her, lying flat on his back as he stared at the ceiling. Eloise turned onto her side and he wrapped an arm around her shoulders, pulling her close, almost absently, it seemed. Was he always like this with a woman after sex? He said the conversation was new, but what about the closeness? Eloise knew she'd never have the courage to ask.

'I can't completely explain it,' Noah said eventually. 'But I'll try.'

'Good enough.' Resting her cheek against his chest, Eloise felt his heartbeat thrumming through her body, in time with her own, and listened.

'When I first saw you…I wanted you, I'll admit that. You're gorgeous, Eloise, whether you know it or not. And there was something about you. I wanted to be close to you. I thought…' He gave a little laugh, low and meek. 'I thought you might be an easy conquest to make the wedding a little more fun.'

'Which I was.' Eloise shrank back at the realisation, but he held her close against him.

'No. No, you were anything but.'

'We're naked in my bed, Noah. I think I've been conquered.' And how easy she'd been for him to claim.

'I think…I think you might have done the conquering,' Noah said after a moment, and Eloise stilled in his arms. 'My agent told me I had to behave this week, if I wanted this director to take me seriously for a big role. No flings. And I tried, I really did. I knew you weren't like the other women I see. You didn't know the rules yet. You saw…more of me. Deeper. And when I kissed you this afternoon…'

When he didn't continue, Eloise said, 'What? What happened then?'

Noah hauled her up his body so she was staring into his eyes, every inch of her pressed up against him.

'When I kissed you, I knew none of it mattered. I couldn't help myself. I knew I had to be with you.'

CHAPTER TEN

HE'D GONE TOO FAR. Noah knew that the moment the words left his mouth. And if he hadn't known the shock in Eloise's eyes would have told him.

'For tonight, I mean,' he said, backtracking fast. 'I couldn't leave Morwen Hall without one night with you.'

'And now you've had it.' Eloise pulled away, and he resisted the urge to tug her close again. He wasn't staying—this wasn't love, wasn't for ever. They both knew that, whatever the crazy attraction between them would have them believe.

'So, what's next for you?' Eloise asked, putting a few inches of blanket between them as she propped her head up on one hand to look at him. 'After you leave Morwen Hall, I mean.'

What was next? He had no idea. He couldn't think beyond this bed, beyond this moment. Beyond her.

'What's this film where the director needs you

to be celibate?' she went on, and Noah breathed a sigh of relief. That was safe. They could talk about the film, about his career. That had to be less perilous than the spiral of feelings sleeping with Eloise had opened up inside him. Or the connection her confessions about her parents had started to foster between them. 'More beating people up and saving the world?'

He huffed out a laugh. 'No, actually. It's more of a relationships movie. About a guy trying to move on after his wife's death. It starts eight days after she dies, and follows him through to eight years later.'

'Sounds deep and meaningful,' Eloise said. 'Both things I thought you tried to avoid.'

'In my personal life? Sure. Professionally…it could be a good move.' Except that wasn't why he was doing it; Noah could admit that to himself, even if he couldn't admit it to her. He needed something more in his life. More than the superficial and the meaningless.

He just wanted to do it on his own terms. That way, at least, he could protect himself from the dangers of feeling too much.

The problem was, when he was with Eloise he

could feel himself wanting more. Suddenly everything he'd always relied on—a fleeting connection, the ability to walk away unchanged—wasn't enough. And the other way lay madness—he knew that from experience.

'You really want this part, don't you?' Eloise asked, and when he turned to her she was watching him too closely.

'How did you know that?' he asked, staring back. He hadn't said how much it mattered to him, hadn't even hinted at anything beyond a professional reason for wanting the role. But Eloise had known all the same.

'I pay attention,' she said. 'So, what is it about this film? Why do you want this part so much?'

'The script is…astonishing. It's the kind of film that wins awards.' But that wasn't all and Eloise seemed to realise that. She stayed silent, waiting for him to say more. 'It spoke to me, I guess. I just knew I had to make this film.'

'The same way you knew you had to have me?' Eloise shook her head, red hair tumbling over her bare shoulders. He remembered pulling the pins out of it one by one and watching it fall loose. The sight of her undone had taken his breath away. It still did. 'This is quite your week for strange, compelling feelings.'

'It is. I blame you.'

She laughed. 'Why? For acting out Shakespeare with you and putting you in touch with your inner Romeo?'

'Because ever since I saw you I've wanted something more than I have.' He inched closer, resting one hand on her waist. 'You know, I spoke to my agent about this part and she told me that if I wanted it I'd need to start looking deeper, start accessing the feelings I've locked away for years.'

'As well as swearing off sex?' Eloise shook her head. 'She's tough. But…maybe she's right.'

'Maybe she is. But that doesn't change the fact that I don't know how. It's been years. But when I met you…I knew you were the sort of person who felt deeply. Who saw deeper, who found meaning.'

'So you thought I could help you get the part?' She frowned. 'I'm really not sure how that would work.'

'That's not it,' Noah said, at a loss for how to explain it. 'I tried staying away from you, but every time I saw you it seemed more impossible.

I tried keeping my distance anyway, tried keeping it just physical. But the moment we kissed… there was more of me in that kiss than in the last ten movies I made.'

'I felt it,' Eloise murmured. 'So why not finish what you started? Look deeper. Feel more. Be the guy you need to be to get that part. I'll listen.'

'I showed you mine; you show me yours?'

'Basically. Isn't that part of what looking deeper means? Dealing with your past? You've heard all my childhood traumas. What are yours? It has to be more than disapproving parents, right?'

Noah's jaw tightened as the memories flooded over him, so intense even after all these years that he worried he might be swept away by them. It felt wrong even thinking about Sally now, here, in bed with Eloise. But he had to admit she was the first woman he'd slept with that he'd ever considered talking to about what had happened.

Could he do it? Should he?

He'd be leaving in a few days. Whatever this connection was between him and Eloise, it would be over the moment he left Morwen Hall. He didn't worry about Eloise spilling all to the Internet, or trying to make money by selling her story. He might have only known her a couple of days but he knew she wasn't that person. Especially now she'd told him about her mother.

Eloise was safe. And if he wanted the part, maybe this was what it would take.

'There was a woman,' he started, then stalled.

'Isn't there always?' Eloise asked sadly. She moved out of his arms and, for a moment, he thought she was going to get out of the cosy, safe cocoon they'd made in her bed. Then she settled against the headboard, still naked, and tugged his arm until he curled up against her side. She settled her arms around him and waited for him to continue.

Noah kissed the top of her breast and rested his head on her shoulder. When was the last time he'd been so *close* to a person, when they weren't actively having sex? Had he ever been? If he had, he couldn't remember it. Not even with Sally...

He was supposed to be telling Eloise all about Sally.

'She was my best friend,' he said eventually.

'The one you moved to LA with?'

'Yes. She was...she was my family, more than

my real family ever were. They didn't understand me or the life I wanted to lead. Sally did.'

'She sounds great.' Noah listened for any hint of jealousy or envy in Eloise's voice, but it wasn't there.

'She was. We got a flat together to start with, but then she met this guy. She'd won a part on a TV show, and he was one of the other actors. She was crazy about him. But he wasn't a good guy. I couldn't put my finger on exactly what it was about him, but I knew he was wrong for Sally.'

'What happened?' Eloise asked. 'And when did you realise you were in love with her?'

Noah sighed. It said something about his levels of emotional understanding that, even seven years later, Eloise knew after five minutes what it had taken Noah years of friendship to realise.

'I think I was always in love with her. Right from the day we met, back at grade school.' She'd walked straight up to him, stuck out her hand and said, 'I'm Sally. You're my new best friend.' And that was all it took. 'But I guess when we hit high school, I realised it for real.'

'And you didn't do anything about it?' Eloise asked, surprise clear in her voice.

'I wasn't Noah Cross, Film Star then, remember. I was nothing. And Sally…she was all I had. The only person in town who understood me— who I was, what I wanted, what mattered to me. I couldn't risk losing that.' The idea of her walking away because she didn't feel the same way had been far too terrifying for him to take the chance.

'So what changed? I mean, I assume something did.'

'Yeah. She moved out of our flat and into his house, and I realised I'd missed my chance.' He'd waited too long and he'd lost her. It had felt like the end of the world—until he'd learned what real loss meant. 'But I figured she was happy, so I should be happy for her. But then she showed up one day with a black eye and I knew I had to get her out of there.'

Eloise stayed silent but her arms tightened ever so slightly around him. He put his hand over hers and squeezed. Even after all this time, the horror he'd felt as he'd seen the bruises marring Sally's perfect skin could still make him feel sick to his stomach.

'I took her home and we talked. She told me it had been going on for months. I couldn't believe

I hadn't noticed. I still can't.' He dipped his head, hiding his eyes from hers. She didn't need to see the shame in them. The guilt. He'd been so busy thinking about himself—about how he felt, what he'd lost, his own emotional turmoil—that he'd missed what was right in front of him and let the woman he loved get hurt. 'She agreed to leave him. And then…'

'You told her how you felt,' Eloise guessed when he didn't continue.

'Yeah.' The feelings were all coming back now, whether he wanted them or not. Those deep, hidden feelings that he'd locked up for so long, because he knew what came next. Knew he couldn't have all that hope and that happiness without the pain that followed. 'Sally…she told me she thought she might feel the same, or that she could one day. We kissed and, just for that brief moment, everything was perfect.' He stopped, just wanting one more moment of that peace, without the fear that snapped at its heels. They lay together in the quiet of the room, listening to the sounds of the hen and stag parties still going on downstairs, and for a moment Noah believed that could be the end of the story.

But then Eloise broke the silence. 'I almost don't want to ask what happened next. But I think I have to.'

With a sigh, Noah pulled away, out of her embrace. Sitting up on the edge of the bed, he stayed facing away from her as he spoke, every word cutting through him as it formed on his lips. 'We agreed to take it slow. We'd already waited so long, and we had our whole future together to figure it all out. The next day, she went back to his house to pack up her stuff while I was out at a call-back audition. I asked her to wait until I could go too, but she wanted to get it done. He was supposed to be at work but…

'I got the part—my first big movie role. I raced home to tell Sally, but when I got there the flat was empty. And then the police called.'

There was a rustle of sheets and then Eloise's body was pressed up against his from behind, her warmth flooding through him as she pressed kisses against his shoulders. But those kisses couldn't erase the guilt he carried every day. He should have been there—not just that day, but every day before that. He should have been looking outwards, not inwards. He should have been there for her.

But he wasn't.

'He'd beaten her. So hard she'd blacked out, they think. And when she fell…her head cracked open on the corner of the table. She died in moments.'

'Oh, Noah, I'm so sorry.' Eloise spoke against his skin, holding him tight to her. 'So, so sorry.'

They were just words, Noah knew. They couldn't fix anything. Couldn't heal the searing pain that had cut through him that day and never fully gone away. His scar tissue might not show on the outside, but it was still there and he felt it pull most days.

But the thing about scar tissue was that it healed thick and hard, and painless. He might feel the tug around it, like healthy skin, but the dead area—his ability to love, to feel those deeper emotions—they didn't hurt at all.

They couldn't.

So he didn't look inwards, not any more. He looked outwards—to easy, casual relationships, to films that focused more on explosions than feelings. And he pushed the guilt and the sorrow down beneath that scar tissue and pretended they weren't there.

Until he'd met Eloise, and read a script that could change his career. And now all those emotions he'd sworn not to feel again were bubbling up, filling him, and he knew he had to beat them back down before they destroyed him.

He couldn't waste emotion on himself. If he had to feel, it would be as a character—safe in another person's fictional life, where the emotions couldn't hurt him. If he felt that pain at all, let it be for the part, for his career. Because Noah Cross didn't deserve to feel any of those things— love, loss, hope—ever again.

'I know I can't say anything,' Eloise whispered, close to his ear. 'I know I can't fix it. But I'm sorry. And whatever you need right now—distance, alcohol, whatever. Just say. I can give it.'

There was only one way to forget, Noah had found, and that was to drown out the memories. Alcohol helped, so did work. But the best thing was sitting naked in bed beside him.

He turned, sweeping her into his arms in one fast movement. 'You,' he murmured against the skin of her neck. 'Let me have you again. Let me forget.'

Eloise nodded, and he bore her down to the bed again, determined to block out the emotions once more.

He'd use them, if he had to. But not as himself. He'd save it all for the part.

He could give Eloise his body, even his memories, but that was all.

Everything else, he'd already given up.

CHAPTER ELEVEN

ELOISE WOKE EARLY, after nowhere near enough sleep to deal with the day ahead. Beside her, Noah slumbered on, one arm wrapped loosely around her waist. She twisted onto her side to look at him, his face peaceful in repose.

In the early morning light, still grey and cold as the sun just started to peep over the horizon, it was hard to imagine all the secrets and wounds they'd shared the night before. After his confession, Noah had made love to her like a man possessed. A man driving out his demons, she supposed.

Did he blame himself for Sally's death? She suspected so, even if he knew intellectually it wasn't his fault. Guilt and grief had a funny way of twisting things in a person's mind.

She felt a tug, somewhere in her middle. A compulsion to try and fix him, to help him feel again. Not just to get some movie role, but be-

202 SLOW DANCE WITH THE BEST MAN

cause he needed it. She'd thought Noah was just another self-centred, narcissistic actor—like her mother. But that wasn't it. He honestly didn't believe that letting people in and feeling something for them could end well. Which, given his experiences, she could sort of understand. She even agreed with him a lot of the time.

But to *always* feel that way... That was a very lonely way to live. Far lonelier even than hers.

She shook her head and prepared to inch out of his arms without waking him.

'Where are you going?' he asked, tightening his hold on her without opening his eyes.

'I thought you were asleep.'

'I was acting.' His eyes opened and he blinked lazily. 'You okay?'

'Sure. Why wouldn't I be?'

'Last night was...intense.'

That was one word for it. Eloise had never experienced anything like it—not the exchange of confidences, or the sex. Everything seemed to be on a higher level with Noah, seemed to strip another layer of her defences away.

'It was,' she admitted. 'I feel...naked, I guess.'

Noah smirked. 'You kind of are.' Hauling her

closer, he angled himself above her again, but there was something different in his passion in the morning light. A desperation she hadn't seen in his eyes before.

'I'm not going to tell anyone, you know,' she said before he could kiss her.

'I know.' His mouth tightened a little and she stretched up to kiss it lightly.

'I want to keep this a secret too, remember.' The last thing she needed was Melissa finding out her latest scandalous story.

Noah frowned. 'Why is that again? Usually I have to stop women shouting from the rooftops after they've slept with me.'

'Really?' Eloise raised her eyebrows and he smiled, the emotions of the night before clearly fading again as he returned to his usual laughing self.

'Well, stop them going to the papers and telling all, anyway. So, why don't you want anyone to know? Is it Melissa?'

'Partly,' Eloise said. How could she put it in a way that wouldn't offend him? 'But it's more than that. I don't want to be another one of your women, with everyone talking about me—and pitying me once you walk away. We both know you're leaving at the end of the week. We have a built-in time limit.'

'I suppose,' Noah said slowly. 'I'm not sure I like being your dirty little secret, though.'

She laughed. 'Who said anything about dirty?'

'I was here last night, remember?' He waggled his eyebrows at her.

'Besides, you're the one who said you wanted a private fling,' Eloise reminded him. 'No strings, no catches—and no gossip.'

'So I'm getting exactly what I want from the situation,' Noah said. 'But what about you?'

'I'm doing okay,' she said, but it was already too late. Noah slid down her body, covering her with kisses and, just for a moment, Eloise let herself imagine having this, having him for longer than a week.

But that way madness lay.

'So, other than *magnificent* sex,' Noah said between kisses, 'what's in it for you?'

Eloise considered, but it was hard to think with his mouth against her skin. 'I like how I feel when I'm with you. Who I am when I'm with you.'

'Yeah?' Noah stilled, resting his head against her hip.

'Yeah.' How could she explain it without adding to his ego? 'I couldn't have done anything like performing on the stage at the Frost Fair without you there, telling me it would be fun. Maybe a few more days with you will give me the confidence I need to move on in my life. Get out of my rut.' Maybe chase the dreams she'd long given up on—her own business, getting away from this place, finding her own success. Maybe even finding a man she could love, who would stay, and want her for who she was. She didn't mention that part, though. Not as Noah began kissing her stomach again.

She wasn't thinking about any man but him for the time being.

By the time Eloise emerged from the pleasurable haze Noah had put her in, the sun was fully up and she was in danger of running late.

'Maybe tonight we can do this in my room,' Noah said as he kissed her goodbye at the door. 'Try out the four-poster.'

Eloise grinned. 'Maybe. Now go! We need to

be downstairs for the wedding party photo shoot and interviews in half an hour.' She pushed him out of the door and he headed off down the corridor, whistling. 'And remember...'

'Nobody knows,' he said, turning and walking backwards. Then he blew her a kiss and she shook her head.

Maybe trusting Noah with a secret relationship was expecting too much from him. As much as he said he wanted it kept between them too, to help convince that director, she wasn't sure he was actually capable of being discreet. But the thought of being in his bed tonight...that was too good to give up. She'd just have to hope he could *act* discreet, just for a few days.

Then he'd be gone. But Eloise wasn't thinking about that.

Instead, as she headed towards her bathroom, she thought that if only she'd known this was going to happen from the start, the bedroom crisis she'd faced on arrival day could have been solved an awful lot more easily.

Thirty minutes later, Eloise hurried from the lift into the lobby. Most of the wedding guests were already milling around, ready to go out on the local tours Laurel had arranged for them while the wedding party were busy with the photographer and the journalist from the celebrity magazine covering the wedding.

'You look nice,' Laurel said as she approached, clipboard in hand, from the reception desk. 'Kind of…glowy.'

'Thanks.' Eloise tried not to blush.

She might have spent just a little more time than normal on her hair and make-up that morning, and put a bit more effort into her choice of suit—a deep charcoal skirt and jacket with a silky cream blouse and high heels. Even though the magazine people would be providing outfits for the photo shoot, and doing her hair and make-up, Eloise had felt like making the effort.

After all, trying to match up to the kind of good looks parading around Morwen Hall at the moment was a full-time job. Nothing to do with the gorgeous guy who'd just spent the night in her bed. Probably.

Oh, who was she trying to kid? She wanted to look nice for her *boyfriend*. That was what Melissa and the other girls would have chanted, back when they were pre-teens at school. But

Noah wasn't her boyfriend. And he wasn't sticking around. Two more days and it would all be over, so there was to be absolutely no falling for the guy.

He'd just stay her own delicious little secret.

Well, not so little, actually.

'Are you okay?' Laurel asked, her eyebrows drawn together in concern. 'You're turning red.'

'Fine. Just fine.' Eloise willed her skin colour to return to normal.

'Well, good. Because Dan and I are off to supervise the coach tours, so you're on your own with Bridezilla today.' Across the lobby, Eloise saw Dan watching, waiting for Laurel, as if he couldn't keep his eyes off her. Obviously a man besotted. Good. Whatever concerns she'd had when she'd first seen them together must just have been nerves—coming out as a couple could do that, she supposed.

Something else she and Noah wouldn't have to worry about. Nobody would ever know about them.

'You're not staying for the photo shoot?' Eloise asked.

Laurel shook her head. 'One of the advantages

of not actually being part of the wedding party. We are surplus to requirements this morning. Plus we'll probably have a lot more fun on the tours.'

'I bet.' The lift pinged behind her and Eloise turned to watch it open, even as she spoke. 'Wish I was coming with you.'

The lift doors opened and Noah stepped out, his dark hair perfectly messy above those dark chocolate-brown eyes, his stubble just the right length for scraping over her skin and his shirt collar open under his jacket, showing hints of the collarbone she'd kissed her way along the night before...

'Are you sure?' Laurel asked, watching her. 'Seems to me you might have your own fun right here.'

'I don't know what you're talking about,' Eloise said, and went to go and see her not-boyfriend.

'Ready for your close-up?' Noah asked as Eloise approached across the lobby.

She certainly looked ready. She'd left her hair down and it tumbled in waves over her shoulders, blazing red against the dark grey of her jacket and the creamy shirt that matched her skin. He wanted to touch it, to touch her. To reach out and kiss her, to show every other person in the hotel that she was his, even if only for a few days.

But he couldn't. Because he'd promised her they'd be a secret, and because one more fling might ruin his chances at getting the film role of the decade.

He knew the reasons. But it still felt like a stupid idea. Anyone who looked at them would know they'd been together, he was sure. At the very least, anyone who'd been paying any attention to Eloise would know she'd been up to something last night. Her whole body screamed relaxed satisfaction, and the smile she gave him told him everything he wanted to know—that they'd be doing it again. And soon.

Thank God. The self-imposed time limit was already weighing heavily on him. In only a few days he'd be gone. That was not a lot of time to make the most of his connection with Eloise Miller.

He didn't let himself consider the possibility of it carrying on beyond New Year's Day. Eloise's life was here, and his was everywhere else. She wanted for ever love, the deep and lasting kind, the sort she could rely on. He wanted anything but that. And, to be fair, she'd not given him any signs that she wanted anything more from their fling. Yes, their connection had been immediate and their chemistry explosive. But just because they'd shared secrets and feelings didn't mean they had to share a life.

Maybe he was destined to only ever have meaningful relationships that lasted a day or two. And maybe that wasn't the worst thing in the world.

At least this time, when it was over, it would be his choice and everyone involved would still be breathing. He'd take that as a win.

'I can't believe they actually want to take photos of me,' Eloise said, standing just an inch or so too close. She wanted to keep this a secret but she didn't even know what she had to hide, Noah realised. Understandably. Eloise wasn't the sort of woman who would have done this before.

'You're the maid of honour,' he pointed out, shifting his weight from one foot to the other to create the illusion of distance between them. 'Kind of important to the wedding party.'

Eloise rolled her eyes. 'I'm the understudy. And

I'm only doing it because Melissa's PR person thought it would look good.'

'And you do look very, very good this morning,' Noah murmured, too softly for anyone else to hear.

Eloise's cheeks flushed the same pink as her skin did after making love. Just the sight of it made Noah want to drag her back off to bed for the rest of the day, photo shoot be damned.

He wasn't quite egotistical enough to believe that the way Eloise was coming out of her shell— performing at the Frost Fair, dressing like she didn't hate everything about her body—was entirely down to sleeping with him. But her words from earlier that morning had stayed with him all through his shower and getting dressed. She liked who she was when she was with him. Not what other people thought of her because she was on his arm, not what being seen with him could do for her career because, if anything, it might damage it, if Melissa really kicked up a fuss.

Just who she was with him.

Noah wasn't sure he'd ever had that sort of an effect on someone before. It was intoxicating.

As the coaches finally left, Eloise led him down

the corridor towards the rooms they were using for the photo shoot and interviews, but as they passed a small, empty office, Noah's willpower ran out. Again.

Tugging her into the office after him, he shut the door and placed his back against it, effectively stopping anyone from interrupting. And her from leaving.

'Noah…' she said as he pulled her into his arms, but any real complaint in her voice was drowned out by the smile spreading over her face.

'What is it about keeping things secret that somehow makes it even sexier?' He kissed his way up her neck and was rewarded with a low moan.

'We've got to go,' Eloise said.

But Noah countered with, 'Just two minutes,' and she gave in rapidly.

Ten minutes later, they finally made it to the photo shoot.

'You're both late,' Melissa said, eyeing them suspiciously.

'My fault,' Noah said cheerfully as he headed towards a clothing rail hung with suits and shirts.

'I overslept after the stag do, so poor Eloise had to come and wake me up.'

Melissa didn't look convinced but, since Eloise had already slunk away to the other side of the room where Caitlin and Iona were both choosing cocktail dresses from a second rail, she at least didn't push the matter.

Noah tried to pay attention to the questions he was being asked by the stylist, and the clothes options in front of him, but it was almost impossible to keep his gaze from Eloise. He found it fascinating, watching her go through the rigmarole of a styling session and photo shoot for the first time. She looked constantly wide-eyed and bewildered and he wanted to be over there, talking her through it, reminding her that being the centre of attention wasn't the worst thing in the world.

But then the real centre of attention—the bride—would glare at him and he'd hear Eloise's voice in his head again, saying, *Nobody knows*, and make a concerted effort to look away.

Even if he didn't last long.

'We're taking shots of all the members of the wedding party in formal dress, to go alongside the photos from the actual wedding tomorrow,' the photographer explained as she positioned Noah where she wanted him, against the backdrop of the main fireplace in the reception area. 'Melissa didn't want there to be any chance of the actual wedding outfits getting out before the big day—understandable, given the amount of money she's being paid for the exclusive—so we just went with some traditional formalwear in complementary colours.'

'Sounds great,' Noah said absently, wondering what Eloise was wearing right now. And how quickly he could get her alone to take it off her.

'If you could just look at me...?' the photographer asked, and Noah brought himself back to the present with considerable effort.

This was part of the job; he knew that. And he needed to give it his full attention.

Once the photos were taken he was whisked off for his interview, where he was asked questions about his friendship with the bride and groom, how he liked Morwen Hall, his latest film, the usual. He smiled, said the right things and kept his guard up just in case the interviewer—a journalist called Sara that he'd worked with a

few times before—slipped in anything contro-
versial. She didn't and, overall, Noah decided
it might have been the most straightforward interview he'd ever had. Apparently not being the
main attraction had its advantages, sometimes.

As he stood to leave, he saw Eloise standing
nervously beside the door to the smaller coffee
bar area they were using for the interviews.

'Want me to stay?' he asked softly. Eloise shook
her head, but Noah was sure that had more to do
with her determination to keep things between
them a secret than because she wanted to do the
interview alone.

Maybe he'd just hang around nearby. Just in
case.

Pouring himself another cup of coffee from the
machine set up on the bar, Noah waved goodbye
to Sara and took his cup just around the corner,
to a high-backed wing chair looking out over
the riverfront. Far enough away that no one was
likely to notice he was there, but close enough
that he'd be able to hear if Eloise got into trouble.
Sure, the questions lobbed at him had been soft
balls, but Eloise wasn't used to this sort of thing.

For a while, things seemed to go well. He

couldn't always make out all the words but Eloise's voice stayed low and even, with a hint of laughter from time to time. She was good, Noah decided, listening intently. Calm and composed, but with enough pauses to show that she was thinking about her answers.

But then, just when Noah had decided they must be wrapping up, Sara threw in one more question.

'I've heard stories that you and Melissa weren't really all that close growing up. That her asking you to step in as maid of honour had more to do with PR than friendship. Do you have anything you'd like to say on that?'

Silence. Placing his coffee cup on the table, Noah peered around the back of his chair, enough to see the alarm on Eloise's face. His body tensed at the sight, desire to save her rising up in him. Without thinking, he got to his feet and crossed to where they were sitting.

'Almost done?' he asked. 'Only I promised Melissa I'd run her maid of honour through her paces again before tomorrow. We have to dance, you see.' He took Eloise's hand and pulled her to her feet. She stumbled and he caught her against his chest, holding her for just a moment too long.

Sara looked between them as Eloise stepped back, not looking at him.

'So, you two must have grown very close, preparing for the wedding together,' she said. 'Anything to all those old sayings about the best man and the maid of honour…?'

Eloise's cheeks flamed red and Noah cursed silently. He should have known better than to get involved, but he just couldn't sit there and watch Eloise struggle.

'I'm sorry,' she said, stepping backwards and almost tripping over the chair. 'I need to go… check the arrangements for the rehearsal dinner.'

And then she was gone, racing out of the bar before either of them could object.

'But I thought you were supposed to be dancing?' Sara asked knowingly.

'So did I,' replied Noah.

CHAPTER TWELVE

THE RESTAURANT WAS blissfully empty when Eloise arrived. The rehearsal dinner wasn't for another few hours, but already the decorations were up, the tables laid and the menus displayed against the festive floral decorations.

Sinking into her assigned seat, Eloise rested her elbows on the crisp white table linen and placed her chin in her hands.

Well.

That had been a disaster.

As much as she'd like to blame Noah for everything, she knew that a large part of the fault lay with her. It was her cheeks that bloomed bright red at the mention of a relationship between her and Noah. Why couldn't she control her body? Of course, if she could she might never have slept with him in the first place.

And, whatever trouble that was likely to get

her into now, she couldn't quite bring herself to regret it.

'Hey,' Laurel called as she walked through the entrance to the restaurant, crossing to where Eloise was slumped at the table. 'Everything ready here? We just got back. Everyone's gone to get changed for the rehearsal dinner. Which I'm guessing you will be doing too...?' She left it hanging, as if she wasn't entirely sure Eloise didn't plan on attending in her suit.

'Yeah.' Eloise glanced at her watch. 'Oh, yes, I'd better get moving. Did the tours go okay? Nice romantic day out with Dan?'

'Yes, thank you,' Laurel said simply. 'What about you? How were the interviews?'

'All fine,' Eloise lied.

'And how is the very gorgeous Noah?' Laurel raised her eyebrows expectantly.

Eloise groaned. 'Don't ask.'

'So there *is* something going on with you two! I knew the gossip was wrong.'

'Gossip?' Eloise jerked her head up. 'What gossip? What are they saying?'

'Nothing bad, I promise.' Laurel pulled out the chair next to Eloise and sat down. 'Nobody's laughing or anything. In fact, everyone seems to think that you're keeping Noah at arm's length. I take it that's not entirely the case?'

'It's a secret,' Eloise blurted out. 'I don't want anyone to know.'

'Well, so far, they don't. In fact, from what I heard, people are pretty amazed. They've seen him hanging around, chasing after you—apparently that's not his usual modus operandi.'

Eloise sat back in her chair and stared at her friend. 'Really? How do you mean?'

Laurel shrugged. 'Seems he usually lets people come to him. He's the chase-ee not the chaser, if you see what I mean.'

Eloise bit her lip, unsure how to feel about this news. Did that mean she meant more than the usual women he dated? After the things he'd said the night before, she'd almost started to hope that she did. Even if this was just a momentary fling, it was nice to know it wasn't meaningless.

But then, was she just fooling herself about that too? They'd been naked in bed at the time. And Eloise knew better than to trust a guy when sex was on the cards. Was it just her poor, inexperienced heart hoping for more?

And, if so, what more was she hoping for? What *more* could there be, really, when he was leaving the day after tomorrow? When no one would ever know what had happened except for him and her.

Well, and Laurel. But she didn't count.

Their whole relationship was a moment out of time. A fantasy.

And maybe the real reason she hadn't been mad at Noah for almost giving them away to the interviewer was that, deep down, she wanted it to be real, in a way it couldn't be if no one knew. Yes, she didn't want to be another of his women, cast aside when he was done with her—that was why keeping this secret was so important.

But if she mattered to him…

No. He'd made it very clear that he couldn't feel that way, couldn't let those deeper feelings in and out, not after Sally. Letting herself believe, even for a moment, that he might care more for her than their short-term fling would allow was dangerous…but exhilarating. Like opening up to him the night before had been—emotionally and physically. And like all the other steps into the spotlight she'd been taking since Noah had arrived.

But letting herself fall in love with Noah Cross was a step too far.

'Are you okay?' Laurel asked and when Eloise looked up she saw her friend was frowning at her. 'You look…scared.'

'I'll be fine.' Eloise pasted on a smile for Laurel's benefit. 'I need to go get ready for tonight.'

And decide how close to the spotlight she was willing to go. Before she got burnt.

Noah went straight from coffee to whisky, once Sara had packed up and departed to get ready for the rehearsal dinner. He'd stayed in the bar near the lobby so he could keep an eye out for Eloise, but there was no sign of her—even when the coaches returned and all the rest of the guests traipsed in.

Unfortunately, in the chaos of people, he also failed to see Melissa approaching.

'Right,' she said, standing beside his chair as the crowd thinned out. 'Time for you and me to have a talk.'

Noah winced and tried to get to his feet, but

apparently the whisky was already working because he felt his head start to spin, then Melissa's hand was on his shoulder, pushing him back down into his seat.

'So. Tell me about Eloise,' Melissa said, taking the seat opposite him. 'Or, more specifically, *you* and Eloise.'

There was no sign of the sweetness-and-light Melissa Sommers who'd been playing to the camera and the media all morning. This Melissa was all business and looked about ready to rip his head off—and Noah was pretty sure it wasn't out of concern for her friend getting hurt.

'There's nothing to tell,' he said with a shrug. The lie came out easily; he was an actor, after all. But, even as he said it, Noah realised he didn't *want* to lie. He wanted to tell the whole world that he was...what? Sleeping with Eloise? *Dating* her, even?

No, he realised. What he really wanted to do was tell the world that Eloise was *his*.

Except she wasn't. At least, not more than temporarily. They hadn't discussed exclusivity because they hadn't had to. Their whole love affair was set to run out in forty-eight hours or less. When would either of them have time to cheat?

If he had more time, he thought he could probably talk Eloise into being open about their relationship—into telling the world, if necessary. She was warming to the spotlight, at least, and getting over her fear of being the centre of attention. And if it was a proper relationship rather than a casual fling, then Stefan, the director, couldn't possibly object—Noah's romantic life would grow boring to the world's media the moment he stayed with one person for more than a week. But time was the one thing he didn't have.

And didn't *want*, he reminded himself. Half of the thrill of his fling with Eloise was knowing they had to make the most of every moment. If he had for ever stretching out in front of him to spend with one woman, he'd be running for the hills. That was just who he was.

Even if that woman was Eloise.

Yes, they'd shared some secrets, and the intimacy had been nice. New, unfamiliar but...comforting, somehow. He'd felt lighter, better, in her arms.

He'd gone deeper with her than with any woman

since Sally. But deep was one thing—falling the whole way was something else altogether.

'I saw the two of you this morning,' Melissa said, her eyes narrow with suspicion. 'If you expect me to believe—'

His phone rang, loud and shrill, on the table, cutting her off. 'I do,' Noah said, picking it up. 'Now, if you'll excuse me? It's my agent.'

Even Melissa had to respect the importance of an agent's phone call. She sat, sulking, in her chair while he got up and paced across the lobby and through the front doors out onto the steps.

'Tessa? What's the news?' The winter air was bitter and Noah huddled against the side of Morwen Hall to stay out of the wind. He figured this weather was still warmer than the chill Melissa was emitting in his direction today.

'Not your love life, for once. Not a hint of an inappropriate sexual encounter anywhere on social media today. I'm impressed.'

'I can show restraint when it matters,' Noah lied. 'Did you get me the video audition?'

'Yes, I got you your call,' Tessa said. 'But they want to talk early this afternoon—evening for you, I guess. You're free, right?'

'Right now, yes,' Noah said. 'But it's the rehearsal dinner for this wedding in an hour or so—'

'Then you'll have to be late,' Tessa interrupted. 'If you really want this part, this is your one chance to convince him.'

Noah took a breath. This was his career at stake. 'What do I need to do?'

'You need to sell it, more than ever before. You need to show them that you get this guy, inside out.' Tessa paused, and Noah knew she was wondering whether he was really capable of it. Ouch. 'Should we talk it through now? Get some ideas going? I've been making some notes…'

'No,' Noah said firmly. 'I've got this. I know this character. I do.'

'So, convince me.' When he didn't answer, she sighed. 'Noah. If you can't sell it to me you're sure as hell not going to sell it to these guys. Then we'll both be on their blacklist for wasting their time.'

'Fine. He's…he's grieving.'

'I think we got that from the dead wife.'

'Yeah, but he's not just grieving for her. He's not just lost a woman he loved. He's lost all hope

that he can ever have that again. He's scared—
so damn scared to take any more risks with his
heart, now he knows how much it can hurt. How
it can destroy you, take you right back to the bone
and leave you to rebuild everything. And when
you do…you're not the same. You can't be. You're
a mass of scar tissue that can't feel anything any
more, and you're *happy* about it. Because at least
it hurts less that way.'

Tessa was silent on the other end of the phone.
Noah grasped for the stone balustrade lining the
steps down from Morwen Hall, desperate for
something to keep him balanced. Grounded.

Because he hadn't been describing a character,
he realised. He'd been talking about himself, the
same way he'd talked to Eloise in bed the night
before. The way he *never* talked.

'Where did that come from?' Tessa asked after
a minute. 'Noah, I've never… Are you okay?'

'I'm fine,' he managed. Then he laughed. 'Let's
just say I've found a new muse.'

'Are actors allowed muses?'

'This one is.' Except he wasn't, not really.
Eloise wasn't his. She was just a temporary distraction.

'Well, whoever she is, hang onto her. Sounds like she's just what you need. As long as you're not sleeping with her,' Tessa said crisply. 'Now, go. Get ready for that call. You've got thirty minutes.'

Time enough to get ready for the rehearsal dinner, so that when he was done with his call he could head straight down there and find Eloise. Not because she was his muse, or because she might be mad at him, or even because she was so sexy he couldn't go another few hours without her again.

Just because he wanted to see her. And because they didn't have much time left.

But Noah intended to make the most of every second.

Eloise smoothed down her cocktail dress as the lift doors opened at the restaurant floor. The dress the stylist had chosen—a beautiful silver and black-edged halter-neck—had looked so good in the photo shoot that she'd asked if she could keep it to wear to the rehearsal dinner that evening. Yes, it was a little more showy than she'd usually wear, but she couldn't wait to see Noah's face when he saw her in it.

If nothing else, it was *definitely* not a boring dress.

She might not be as beautiful as Melissa, in her pale pink gown that showed off every curve and slender line of that famous body, and she knew she couldn't live up to the beauties Noah usually had on his arm. But, in this dress, Eloise felt beautiful in herself. And that was enough for her.

The restaurant floor was already buzzing by the time Eloise arrived. Whereas a more normal wedding might just have a rehearsal dinner for the wedding party and family members, Melissa and Riley had wanted a wedding extravaganza and that was what Laurel and Eloise had given them. For the rehearsal dinner—ignoring the fact they hadn't actually *had* a rehearsal of the wedding itself because Melissa said she'd played a bride on screen often enough to know what to do—they were holding another drinks reception in the bar area, then a special dinner for all the guests in the restaurant. The wedding party, along with Melissa and Riley's families, would then retire to a private room, where they could do the usual speeches and gift presentations.

'Now *that* is a dress.' Noah's voice, warm and appreciative, behind her, was already so familiar that Eloise smiled even as she turned to face him.

'Somehow, I had a feeling you might like this one.'

'I do.' He raked his gaze up and down her body and for once Eloise didn't even blush. He'd seen more, after all. 'It looks fantastic on you.'

'But let me guess.' Eloise leant closer to keep her words private. 'It would look better off.'

Noah met her gaze and smiled, and Eloise knew there was a promise in that smile. 'That goes without saying.'

'You're in a good mood,' Eloise said, taking in his sparkling eyes.

'I just gave the best audition of my life, over video chat.'

'For the part? *Eight Days After*?'

'That's the one.' Noah grinned again, as if he couldn't quite bring himself to stop. 'If they don't give me the part after that, then they never would have. I gave it everything and was pretty darned good too.'

Eloise wondered what it must be like to live with that sort of self-confidence, even if only in a professional sphere. 'You found a way to go deeper, then?'

'Yes.' His expression dropped into something more serious, but so compelling Eloise couldn't have looked away if she'd wanted to. 'You. You helped me talk about Sally, helped me examine what *I* felt back then, so I could transfer it to the character. I'd been putting off dealing with that for a long time.'

'I'm not sure one conversation counts as dealing with it,' Eloise warned. Grief was a tricky thing—especially when it had been blocked and ignored as long as Noah's had.

'But it's a start,' he said. 'And I have you to thank for it. However can I repay you?' His lips curved up into a smile again, but this one felt more intimate. More seductive.

'I have some ideas...' she said.

Noah leant in, just a little more, and in a flash Eloise remembered where they were—in the middle of the bar, surrounded by celebrities and at least one photographer. She pulled back, and spotted Melissa watching them from across the room. She didn't look happy.

'Time to mingle.' Eloise gave him an apologetic smile. 'But I'll see you later?'

'Most definitely.' She felt Noah's eyes on her as she walked away and she knew, deep down, he was definitely imagining her naked. And she loved knowing that.

She spent the drinks reception chatting with the other guests, many of whom she'd failed to speak to at all before then—a side effect of being so caught up with Noah, she supposed. Since many of them just expected her to nod and smile politely as she listened to them regale her with their best stories of celebrity life, she had plenty of time left for daydreaming about the night ahead, once she and Noah were alone again.

Tonight, there would be no secrets between them. No emotional outpourings and confessions.

Just them, and one perfect night before the wedding from hell.

She couldn't wait.

Eventually, it was time for the party to move through to the restaurant for the dinner. Eloise groaned inside when she spotted the menu, and remembered that Melissa had wanted a seven-course tasting menu, with matching wines. Add in the speeches and the gifts for the groomsmen and bridesmaids and it would be hours before she could escape with Noah.

Then she saw him, sitting beside her place at the table, and realised there was no way she was going to make it that long.

'You switched the place settings,' she whispered as she slid into her seat. 'Melissa will be mad.'

'It's worth it,' Noah replied. 'I'm not taking the chance of another groomsman seducing you away from me while you're wearing that dress.'

'You get very territorial over your flings, don't you?'

'Not usually.' Noah frowned just a little, then glanced around to make sure no one was listening. Leaning in, he murmured, 'Look, I reckon I can make it through maybe two of these taster courses before I have to have you again. So, when I leave, wait a couple of minutes and follow me, okay?'

Heat flared through Eloise's body. Just knowing he wanted her as much as she needed him was an incredible aphrodisiac. Still, the more sensible part of her brain was screaming that this was a stupid idea. It was the rehearsal dinner! They would definitely be missed, and Melissa would be furious if she realised where they'd gone...

She should say no. She *had* to say no.

'Okay,' she whispered, and Noah smiled.

A storage cupboard wasn't exactly high on Noah's list of Most Seductive Spots, but right now he'd take what he could get. Sitting next to Eloise in that dress and not touching her—not even a hand on her back or a kiss on her cheek—had been physically painful.

And okay, fine. It wasn't the dress that was causing the problem.

It was her.

In lots of ways, it was just as well that in two days' time there'd be thousands of miles between them. Any less and he'd be tempted to hurry back and have her again, regardless of the rules.

He just hoped five thousand miles would be enough.

Time passed excruciatingly slowly as he waited to hear Eloise's footsteps in the corridor outside.

Surely it had to have been three minutes since he'd left the table? He'd chosen the cupboard for its proximity to the restaurant, and the fact he could see out the crack of the open door to watch for Eloise. Any further away and he'd run the risk of her not finding him. And that was not an option.

But right now he had to think about something else. Imagining Eloise was driving him insane, and if he didn't slow down that dress she looked so incredible in wouldn't survive its first encounter with his hands.

Think about the film. The audition. Noah smiled in the darkness. The director had pretty much offered him the role on the spot, he'd been so impressed. Noah had managed to channel all those emotions he'd been repressing into the part, just as he'd planned. And, yes, it had stung—but it wasn't quite so painful when it was a character feeling those things instead of himself. He could do it, he knew now. He'd do the part justice; he'd win that award—and he could move on and leave all the awful pain and emotion behind him when he did.

Stefan had reiterated Tessa's point about how

important it would be to keep his personal life low-key, so the focus would be on the film not the stars, and Noah had agreed readily. Whatever he had with Eloise would be over soon enough and afterwards…he didn't think he'd be hurrying into anything else for a while. He could take a break.

He'd dropped Tessa an email to let her know how it went, then hurried straight down to the rehearsal dinner to tell Eloise, to celebrate with her.

And what a celebration he had planned…

Apparently it was impossible to think about anything but her.

Finally, the restaurant door swung open and Eloise stepped out, her cheeks flushed with more than just wine, he was sure. She'd sat so tense beside him at dinner, he was certain she'd been resisting her urges almost as hard as he had.

It was hard to imagine that when he'd first met her he'd thought her reserved and stand-offish. Maybe with others. But with him she was a free spirit, giving everything she got and more.

He waited until Eloise was about to walk past the cupboard, then reached out a hand and dragged her inside. She squeaked with surprise, but then her hands were slipping under his jacket and up his back so he didn't think she was too traumatised.

'That was excruciating,' she murmured against his neck, as he lifted her to rest against a conveniently located pile of boxes.

'You're telling me.' He nudged her knees open with his hips and stepped between them, pressing up against her body. 'I almost didn't make it past the first course.'

'I noticed.' Her hands moved round to the front and unbuttoned the top few buttons of his shirt, and she leant in to kiss along his collarbone. 'I thought you were going to drag me out of there ten minutes ago. Or maybe just take me on the table, in front of everyone.'

'Not very secret, that.' He slid his hands up her bare thighs.

'No, not very secret.'

For a moment he held his breath, waiting for her to say something more. To say it didn't have to be a secret. To say that she wanted the whole world to know about them. That she didn't care what Melissa or anyone else said about them. That she trusted him not to let them mock her in the press.

But she didn't. And she shouldn't. Because that wasn't the deal they had. It wasn't even what he wanted really, logically.

This was a fling. That was what she'd asked for, what he'd promised.

So that was what he had to give her.

Even if he was starting to feel as if he wanted more.

As if he wanted everything.

'I've never had sex in a cupboard before,' she murmured against his ear, and Noah dragged himself back to focus on what he *could* have. Eloise, here and now, wanting him. 'You're providing me with all sorts of new experiences this week.'

'I'm a full service secret fling,' Noah said, untying the back of her halter-neck and lowering the zip to reveal her bare breasts. 'No bra?'

'Seemed like a waste of time.' Eloise gasped as he dipped his head to kiss her.

'Agreed,' he said when he came up for air. 'Now, let's see what else you're not wearing under this—'

A flash of light cut him off as the cupboard door he was leaning against opened, sending him tumbling into the hallway, pulling Eloise with him. He blinked at another flash and saw Melissa, Sara the journalist and her photographer standing over them.

And suddenly nothing was secret any more.

CHAPTER THIRTEEN

ELOISE YANKED HER dress back up, trying to make herself respectable again, even though the sinking feeling inside told her it was already far too late.

Scrambling to his feet, Noah pushed her behind him, giving her the cover she needed to fix her dress. But his shirt was still open, exposing exactly what they'd been doing.

Not that anyone could be in any doubt after that display.

What had she been thinking? She'd *known* this was a terrible idea from the start. But then Noah would say something to convince her and there she'd be, half naked in a cupboard.

Or outside a cupboard. With her teenage nemesis arching her eyebrows and the world's media taking photos.

'Well, really,' Melissa said too loudly, her words echoing off the walls. 'Some people just don't know how to behave at a respectable wedding, do they?'

Eloise wanted to ask her to keep it down before anyone else heard and came out to investigate, but that was probably why Melissa was doing it in the first place, she realised. She hadn't managed to keep Eloise and Noah apart, so she'd decided to go the other way. If they were intent on stealing the limelight at her wedding, she was going to ruin them.

Abject humiliation. Melissa wouldn't settle for anything less than making sure Eloise's whole world knew who she was and what she'd done— the same way she had when they were teenagers and the guy Melissa had a crush on asked Eloise out instead. Soon, the whole school knew every story about Eloise's mother and believed that she was just the same and the guy never spoke to her again.

The only difference was that this time Melissa had made sure the actual whole world would know, through the power of the media and the Internet.

Never mind the humiliation Eloise's mother's antics had brought her over the years, this was a million times worse. And the most awful part was that she'd done it all herself. There was no one to blame except her own suddenly overactive libido…and the secret part of her heart that hoped to be something more than a fling to someone like Noah Cross.

She'd had ideas of her own importance, her own entitlement to the spotlight—and now she'd been burned.

'Melissa, come on,' Noah said, laughing lightly as he tried to reach for the photographer's camera. She stepped back out of his reach and Eloise knew that no one in their right mind would give those photos up. Noah Cross, caught in the act? That had to be worth a fortune.

And nobody would care if her reputation was shredded in the process.

She had to get out of there. She had to get a million miles away from this spotlight, right now.

'I have to go.'

Holding her dress in place, she pushed past Noah and the others and ran towards the lifts. She could hear him behind her, calling her name, making excuses, but she couldn't turn back, couldn't listen.

This wasn't her world, even if Noah and Melissa's celebrity lives had infiltrated Morwen Hall. Soon they'd be gone and she could get back to quietly living down her mother's reputation. To her responsible, boring, staid and lonely existence.

It had to be better than the shame and humiliation burning through her right now.

Noah watched Eloise run away and had to force himself not to chase after her. She didn't want this—she'd made that clear from the start.

This was his fault. She'd wanted secret and in his desperation he'd ruined that.

And now he had to fix it.

'So, Noah. Any quote to go with our pictures?' Sara asked, holding out her phone and showing it was recording. Another part of his life on the record.

He'd wanted to tell the world about him and Eloise. But not like this.

Stefan. The part. He'd promised he wouldn't do this, promised he'd keep things low-key. And this was pretty much the opposite. The role he'd thought he had nailed—this could ruin everything. Send him back to playing brainless action figures for another seven years. Unless he could convince people that things with him and Eloise were serious, something more than a fling. Maybe then he'd get a second chance from Stefan...

The idea was intoxicating. He could play at love with Eloise, enjoy what they had for a little longer, until it came to its natural conclusion when no one cared and the world wasn't watching. He could still have everything he wanted if Eloise went along with it, if he lied... He could turn this round, still be the good guy maybe.

But first he had to get a handle on himself, on all the emotions rushing through him at the speed of light. As if, after spending so many years not feeling them, now he'd let them in they were making up for lost time. Embarrassment, fear, anger, lust—they all surged through him, swirling around into a toxic mix that left him close to losing it.

No. He wasn't that man. He'd never been the celebrity yelling at reporters or causing a scene. He wouldn't start now—not least because it would only make things worse for Eloise, and he couldn't do that to her.

Cold realisation flooded through him. The only thing he could really do now was protect Eloise. Even if it meant giving up on the part he wanted so much. Because he couldn't promise her for ever, couldn't ask her to act out a sham relationship. Couldn't break her heart a few months down the line when she realised that what she saw really was all he had to give—there was nothing deeper.

He couldn't hurt her any more than he had to. And the only way through this with minimum casualties was to lessen the impact of what had happened.

Which meant pretending it was nothing at all.

He couldn't do it—couldn't pretend what he and Eloise had was nothing. It might not be everything but it was *something*. He couldn't deny Eloise that way, not after everything she'd done for him.

Except he was doing this *for* her. So he had to.

Maybe he couldn't. But Noah Cross, celebrity, notorious womaniser and charmer could.

It took only a second to switch on the character—the one he'd been playing since the day Sally died. It was so familiar that, until this week, he might even have said it was the real him.

But it wasn't. He knew that now. He'd found the person he was underneath all that scar tissue. He just wasn't sure if he'd ever let him out again, except for when he was in character.

'What is there to say?' he said with a shrug and a crooked smile. 'You know how it is at weddings. All that romance in the air. A fling always makes it a little more entertaining, right?' He cringed inside as he remembered saying the same thing to Eloise at the welcome drinks. Could that really have only been two days ago?

'So, it's nothing serious is what you're saying,' Sara pressed.

Noah forced himself to laugh, to sound as light-hearted and as uncaring as he *should* be about the situation, trying not to think what Stefan would think. 'Sara, I'd think you—and the rest of the world—know me a little better than that by now.'

'So, just business as usual for Noah Cross then,' Sara said. 'Another wedding, another woman.'

'Basically.' This felt so wrong. Even though he was only telling the truth, saying what he and Eloise had agreed should be the case, he could tell by the creeping sense of shame filling him that something had changed.

Eloise wasn't just a fling. Wasn't just another woman.

Except she had to be. And he needed to rebuild his walls to keep her behind them before he left.

Especially if he wanted to save her from a mauling in the media and Melissa's wrath.

'She's nothing to me,' he lied, 'and I'm nothing to her. Just a spot of fun. Now, if you'll excuse me...' He started to move towards the elevators, hoping to catch up with Eloise, but Melissa grabbed his arm and dragged him around the other way.

'Absolutely! We've got a rehearsal dinner to finish, remember, best man?'

'Right.' Noah smiled weakly and went back to work.

Eloise would have to wait.

Another night with no sleep, Eloise thought as the sun peeked over the horizon the next morning, hazy behind the grey winter clouds. And this time for far less satisfaction than the night before.

She hadn't had the courage to go back to the rehearsal dinner, although she suspected Noah had. She'd heard him banging on her door around midnight, asking her to let him in, but she'd ignored him. Maybe he'd thought she was asleep, or angry, or out. She didn't care. Eventually he'd grown tired and left her in peace.

Not that it had been very peaceful.

She'd stripped off that wretched dress and curled up in her warmest, softest pyjamas, make-up removed and hair brushed out. She'd cocooned herself in her duvet and tried to forget, tried to sleep. But every time she closed her eyes all she could see was that camera flash and Melissa's arched eyebrows.

How could she have been so stupid? How could she have put herself in a position to let Melissa humiliate her all over again? Melissa always had to be the queen bee, had to have the highest profile. It was her wedding. Of course she was going to obsess about it being all about her. And, yes, she had Riley—hot up-and-coming star. But in Melissa's world Noah was a bigger catch, one who'd eluded capture by every woman in Hollywood. Of *course* she was going to freak out about Eloise—sad, quiet little Eloise—sleeping with him. At her *own* wedding.

She was an idiot. All she'd needed to do was keep the lid on her libido until the wedding was over. How hard would that have been?

Eloise sighed. Impossible, apparently.

Eventually, she'd given up on sleep and logged onto the Internet on her tablet, refreshing Sara's magazine pages until the exclusive she'd known was coming flashed up on the screen at last.

There she was. Eyes wide from the camera flash, her hand wrapped over her chest covering her nudity. Noah lay underneath her on the floor, then in later photos stood in front of her, looking mussed but gorgeous. Charmingly contrite having been caught, his shirt open a little too far, his hair ruffled beyond the usual fashionable mess. He could have stepped out of an advert for aftershave, not been caught falling out of a cupboard moments before having sex.

Whereas she... There was no doubt what she'd been doing. She looked exactly the type of girl Melissa had always told people she was.

Why could men get away with that sort of behaviour and women couldn't?

Bracing herself, Eloise scanned down through all the photos to the text underneath.

Since half of Hollywood has decamped to England for the wedding of Melissa Sommers and Riley Black, we can report exclusively from Morwen Hall on all the wedding high jinks! Starting with this gem from the rehearsal dinner—best man Noah Cross has found some entertainment to make the week even more fun than Melissa and Riley planned: seducing the maid of honour!

It went on to detail who she was, how she knew Melissa and why she'd stepped in at the last minute.

Then it got to what really mattered.

So could this be true love for eternal bachelor Noah? Apparently not.

He said, 'She's nothing to me, and I'm nothing to her. You know how it is at weddings... A fling always makes it a little more entertaining.'

Looks like we'll have to wait a little longer to see Noah walk down the aisle himself!

Eloise threw her tablet down onto the covers and wished she'd never looked.

Of course he'd said that. He'd never suggested anything else—in fact he'd said practically the same thing to her at the welcome drinks. She'd known what she was getting into. Like he'd told her the night before—he never gave his women false expectations, never fell for them, and never ever told them he loved them.

He played fair. It was only her heart that had cheated.

She'd been so sure that she could play the same game he did, that it wasn't the same as her mother's games if no one mentioned love. But, in the end, she'd ended up exactly where all her mother's men had: alone, heartbroken, her reputation in tatters and everyone talking about her. It was exactly the way she'd felt after she'd found her mother sleeping with her boyfriend, or the day she'd realised that her university boyfriend had been using her all along—stupid, naive, gullible and humiliated.

She was just where she'd always promised herself she'd never be again. And all thanks to Noah Cross.

Because she'd let herself believe, just for a moment, that what they had could be something
more than either of them had promised each
other. That it could be for real—not a secret, not
a fling, not anything to hide or be ashamed of.

And that moment was all that it took for her to
fall head over heels in love with Noah.

Closing her eyes, Eloise fell back against the
bed and swore softly. Turned out she really was
every bit as stupid and naive as Melissa had always told her she was.

Noah awoke feeling worse than any hangover
had ever left him and he hadn't drunk more than
a glass of wine the night before. He'd stuck the
rehearsal dinner out until the bitter end, flinch-
ing when Melissa told the guests that Eloise had
gone to bed with a headache. By midday they'd
all know exactly why she'd gone to bed, he knew,
but at least the lie had preserved her peace and
dignity for a few more hours.

He'd tried to speak with her after the dinner
but there'd been no answer at her door. He hoped
she'd been sleeping, but knew it was far more

likely she'd been avoiding him. Well, she couldn't do that for ever.

Forcing himself out of bed, Noah dressed quickly and headed straight for Eloise's room. He needed to speak to her before anyone else did. Hopefully before she saw the photos on the Internet, for that matter—although, since he'd already had a furious voicemail from Tessa, ranting about him throwing away his chances that morning, that was probably a long shot.

'Eloise?' He didn't want to shout—he knew that attracting more attention to them could only make everything worse—but when she didn't answer his third knock he had to raise his voice. 'Let me in, Eloise.'

There was a shuffling noise inside, then she yanked the door open, looking furious under her rumpled red hair. She was wearing what had to be the most unflattering pair of pyjamas in history and Noah realised that it didn't even matter. She had bags under her eyes as if she hadn't slept, and mascara on her cheeks, and her pyjamas had pictures of grumpy cats on them, and he still wanted her.

Eloise, however, did not look like she was having the same problem.

'What are you doing?' she whisper-shouted at him. 'Do you want even more people showing up to take photos of me half dressed?'

Noah decided not to point out that the cat pyjamas covered considerably more of her body than last night's dress. 'Can I come in?'

Eloise scanned the hallway and, finding it empty, stood aside, still glaring at him.

'Look, we both have a wedding to get ready for in four hours,' she said, shutting the door behind him. 'So, whatever you have to say, make it quick.'

She folded her arms over her chest and stared at him, and all of Noah's intended words fled. He'd planned to talk about how they could minimise the fallout from last night, how to deal with Melissa today...but instead he found himself saying, 'I'm sorry. About last night. I know that was the last thing you wanted.'

'I'm not sure many people want to be caught half naked in a cupboard, Noah.'

'You'd be surprised.' If it meant getting their photo taken with him, Noah had found that some women were willing to do anything. But Eloise wasn't one of them.

She shot him a disgusted look. 'Of course. I'm sure your many admirers would be grateful for the chance.'

'That's not what I meant.'

'I don't care.' She rubbed one eye with her fist and he realised again how exhausted she looked. Had she slept at all? 'Look, I've already seen the photos online, read all the quotes. So kind of you to point out that I was equally indifferent to you, by the way, since, after all, I mean nothing to you.'

Noah winced. 'I'm sorry, okay? I was trying to downplay it all for your sake! You're the one who didn't want to be another woman cast aside and presumably heartbroken when I left them. *You* wanted to keep it a secret. And, since that was off the table…I figured that this was the next best thing.' He'd given up his chance at the movie role of a lifetime to try and protect her, and this was the way she thanked him?

Eloise stared at him so long he started to worry he'd grown an extra head while he'd slept. 'Did you honestly believe that telling them I was just a meaningless fling would *help*?'

'You're the one who insisted that nobody know!' Couldn't she see he'd done the best he could in a bad situation? 'We both agreed this wasn't anything serious. Just a fling to kill a few days, right? Get the chemistry out of our system. That's what we *agreed*.' They'd had a deal and he'd stuck to it. He'd *protected* her—at his own expense! So why was he the bad guy?

And why was Eloise staring at him so sadly, her eyes huge and wet and her cheeks pale?

'You're a fool if you still believe that,' she said softly.

Noah's whole world tilted, for the second time since he'd met Eloise. What was it about her that kept him permanently off balance? 'What?'

He could see her throat move as she swallowed, as if she was preparing herself for something hard. Something she didn't want to do.

'I know what we agreed, what we said. I was there too.' She met his gaze head-on and he felt it down to his core, past all those carefully built defences he'd put back up. As if they didn't exist for her at all. 'But I want more. And I think you do too. Being with you…it's so different to anything I've ever had before.'

'Well, yeah,' he said awkwardly. 'I mean, it would be. My world, the way I live…it's a new experience for you, I get that. You've been hiding out in this hotel for so long…'

Eloise shook her head violently. 'That's not what I'm talking about and you know it. I don't care that you're a movie star. I don't care that you're famous or rich or in demand or even that you're leaving tomorrow. I care that you spoke to me like you trusted me…that you listened to me when I told you my secrets. I care that you made me see it was okay to come out of my shell, to try new things, to let people see the real me. I care that when you touched me…my whole world lit up.'

'That's just sex.' The defence was automatic. Sex he knew. Sex was safe. The other stuff… Any of that he still had left he needed to save for his next movie role—if he got one that was worth anything at all after this. 'And the talking… I told you. I wanted to get this part and they needed me to act deep.'

'Are you honestly trying to tell me that everything between us happened because you wanted to win some role in a film?' She raised her eyebrows as she stared at him, and he knew it was crazy. Knew that what had happened between them transcended not just his career but his life so far.

And that was why it scared the hell out of him. He'd had something close to this once—and he'd lost it the moment he'd admitted to it.

He wasn't taking the chance of feeling that pain again.

'You know us actors,' he said, shrugging as casually as he could. 'We'll do anything for a shot at an award.' Not that he had a hope of that now—but Eloise didn't need to know that. If she realised what he'd given up trying to protect her she might read something more into it than there was.

Her mouth actually dropped open. A director would tell her she was overacting, but Noah knew better. Eloise didn't act. She was who she was, and it was glorious.

But he knew something else too. She didn't believe she was worth it, and he could use that now. Because looking deeper was one thing. Falling in love was another altogether—it would take him all the way into his soul and out the other side and it could burn him up on the journey. If he wanted to hold onto Eloise, that was what he knew it would take—everything.

And he didn't have it in him any more.

'You know, the saddest thing is, you might really believe that,' Eloise said, her voice soft. 'You might actually believe that you're just an actor and it's all just a role. But you're wrong. I saw the real you, I know it. And I think we could have been happy. I don't know how it would have worked, or what would have happened next, but we'd have been happy. And it doesn't matter now because you won't even try. You won't let yourself feel anything as real and as deep as love. Even if it could give you everything that's been missing for the last seven years.'

'You're wrong,' he said but, even as the words came out, he knew he was lying.

He could have been happy.

But how long for?

'I'll see you at the wedding,' he said. And then he turned and walked out on love. For good.

CHAPTER FOURTEEN

'TOLD YOU SHE wouldn't wear the veil.' Laurel sidled up to Eloise as they stood outside the ceremony room, waiting for the signal to start the procession. Caitlin and Iona were fussing with Melissa's train while the bride checked her reflection one last time and straightened the tiara on her—veil-less—head.

'You were right,' Eloise said, viewing the proceedings with a strange detachment. As if she were watching the action on a cinema screen, not really part of it at all.

Quite a lot of the last few days seemed like that now, actually.

'You okay?' Laurel asked, lowering her clipboard and looking up at her, concern in her eyes. 'I heard… Well, there's been a lot of talk this morning.'

'I'm sure there has,' Eloise replied serenely. Of course there would be. Everyone staying at Morwen Hall would have woken up to the comedy gold that was her falling out of a cupboard half naked with Noah Cross.

But at least they didn't know the worst of her humiliation. Noah was right about that—he'd defended her from the mortification of everyone in the world knowing that she'd fallen in love with Noah and been rejected. They were the only two people in the world who knew exactly what had happened between them that week.

In a way, their fling was still a secret. Others might speculate but they'd never know the truth of it.

That mind-set was the only thing that had got her through Melissa's snide comments and the half jokes and sniggers from the other bridesmaids as they'd got ready together that morning. The make-up artist Melissa had hired had tutted and despaired aloud at the bags under Eloise's eyes, but some serious application of concealer and other potions from her magic bag of tricks seemed to have hidden them well enough. The icy blue-green dress had been laced tight enough to give her some semblance of curves and her red hair curled and pinned up on the back of her head, leaving her neck bare.

Eloise couldn't help but feel as if she'd been prepared for an execution.

'You seem very…calm,' Laurel said. 'Serene, even.'

Eloise gave her a small smile and raised one shoulder in a half shrug. 'What else is there to do?'

'I suppose.'

She'd realised after Noah left, after she'd wailed and sobbed and thrown things at the door he'd left through, that this was it. The lowest she could go. The whole world knew everything about her that she'd wanted to keep secret, and they probably all thought the worst. Either she was a fame-hungry slut seducing Noah in a cupboard, or a crazed fan lusting after him and thinking herself in love, when he was just using her for a bit of light relief.

But the thing was, neither of those were true. They were all an act—every theory, every story.

And, underneath them all, she was still Eloise Miller. Still in love with Noah Cross. Not the film star, but the man.

And no amount of humiliation could hurt as much as knowing that after today she might never see him again.

But he'd given her something, at least. She knew now what she needed to do next. He'd been right about one thing, somewhere in the middle of all his lies. She'd been hiding away at Morwen Hall for too long—too scared to go after her own dreams, to risk stepping into the spotlight and fighting for what she really wanted.

She'd fought for Noah. She might not have won him but she'd taken the risk and told him the truth—that she loved him. That was a big step.

And as soon as this wedding was over she would take another one. She'd hand in her notice at Morwen Hall and step out of hiding at last. It was time to go after all those other dreams she'd been too scared to chase—her own company, a career she could feel passionately about. Her own life, somewhere else.

She had a lot of planning to do, Eloise knew. But if she took nothing else away from her encounter with Noah Cross, she would have this: she wasn't afraid of the spotlight any more.

How could she be? After all, it couldn't ever get

worse than this. And that thought was strangely liberating.

The string quartet at the front of the ceremony room started a new piece and Melissa gave a little squeal. 'It's time!'

'Good luck,' Laurel whispered as they lined up in their assigned order. 'I'm going to head in and watch from the front.'

Eloise nodded to show that she'd heard her, but otherwise kept her focus on the task at hand. All she had to do was get through the rest of the day, and then she could fall apart and start again. Just another ten hours until the clock ticked past midnight and they entered a whole new year.

A fresh start. Just what she needed.

The doors opened and Eloise took her first careful, measured step, her bouquet held up at just the right height, right foot first, as instructed.

They'd opted to hold the ceremony in the old ballroom—one of the few rooms inside the hotel that retained some of the original Gothic charm. The high, peaked windows let in the winter light through thick glass, glinting off the displays of bright white flowers on every sill. The chairs the hotel staff had laid out in neat rows were now filled with the rich and famous, and at the end of the long aisle stood the celebrant, flanked by Riley, the groom, and Noah. The best man. The only man for her.

And the one man she was certain she could never have.

Eloise concentrated on her breathing as she made her way steadily down the long aisle, ignoring the whispers and muffled laughs around her. Then she heard the gasps and 'ah's as she reached the halfway point and knew that Melissa had made her entrance too. Nobody cared about Noah Cross's fling any more. Melissa was the main attraction—just as she should be, and just as she'd wanted.

Eloise was more than happy to give up *this* spotlight to her.

As she approached the celebrant, Noah turned at last and she focused on not losing control as she saw his face. He didn't look like his life had just been ripped apart—probably because it hadn't.

Was it really all just an act for him? All that they'd shared, could it really have only been a means to an end? She didn't want to believe it, but maybe she should. He was an actor. He was everything she'd always suspected he would be. Even all he'd shared about Sally—maybe it was just a sob story designed to get her into bed.

Except she'd already been in bed.

And except that it had felt real.

Eloise might not be very well acquainted with love, but now she'd felt its effects, a small part of her couldn't give up the hope that maybe he felt it too.

Noah looked right at her and Eloise dropped her gaze. She couldn't let him see how badly he'd hurt her. Despite everything, she still had her pride.

But then something made her glance up again to study his face, just for a moment—and she *knew*.

Noah Cross was a brilliant actor. But even he couldn't out-act love.

The only problem was, love didn't make a blind bit of difference if he wouldn't let himself feel it. He probably didn't even know himself.

Which meant that Eloise was no better off than she'd been when he'd left her bereft that morning. In fact, she might be worse.

Because now she knew that *both* of them were

going to lose what might have been the most important thing in their lives.

The ceremony was excruciating. Not just watching Melissa and Riley pledge undying love, when everyone in the room knew it probably wouldn't last five years. In fact, when he'd arrived there had been someone at the back of the room giving odds.

Noah hadn't placed a bet. He didn't bet on love these days.

No, the worst part had been the way Eloise wouldn't meet his eyes—except for the one brief moment when she'd frowned at him, as if seeing something she didn't expect. He'd wanted to ask her what she thought she'd seen, what depth she thought he'd sunk to now. But the room was full of eyes and, besides, even if they hadn't been in the middle of a wedding, he'd given up that right when he'd walked out on her that morning.

'Dearly beloved, we are gathered here today...' The celebrant droned on, using the movie script version of the wedding ceremony that Noah suspected they'd paid extra for. This wasn't a marriage, wasn't a declaration of love. It was the ultimate act—a chance for Melissa and Riley to show the rest of the world what they didn't have, not realising how much more some couples *did* have. True love. A connection that couldn't be broken by failing box office receipts. A partner they could rely on. Someone to grow old and grey with, not plan plastic surgery with.

Someone who saw into their soul, and loved them anyway.

He bit the inside of his cheek to force himself to stop thinking about it, as he handed the rings over to Riley. What did it matter to him how shallow this whole day was? It wasn't as if he was searching for anything deeper. He wasn't even willing to get as far as a third date, let alone the altar. He had no moral high ground here.

Suddenly, the room erupted into applause and Noah realised he'd missed the 'I do's and everything that went with them. Moments later, they were all parading back out of the ballroom, ready to have photographs taken to immortalise this very special day in print and online, while the rest of the guests got to eat canapés.

He wanted to go and stand by Eloise, to tell her jokes until she looked less…absent. She looked as if she'd mentally checked out of the whole day already. Not that he could blame her. He'd heard enough of the talk that morning—and, as expected, it was all about her. No one expected anything else from him, he supposed.

No, even if she didn't just slap him the moment he got close, he couldn't do anything to make this day any harder for her. It just felt wrong, watching her try to fade into the background, to disappear at the celebrity wedding of the year. She belonged in the spotlight, whatever she believed. She was so vibrant, so bright, so real. That was what the world should be looking at, not the superficial and the showy.

The world should be looking at Eloise the way he was. As if she was the most important person on the planet. She deserved no less.

He wanted the world to see what real love looked like. Not fake Hollywood romance like Melissa and Riley's. Not him and whichever woman he took out that night. Real love—the sort that had shone out of Eloise like a holy truth that morning, when she'd told him she loved him.

The world should see that. And they should see it returned. They should see the truth of his feelings—the way his soul felt lighter when she smiled at him, the way his life lit up when she was beside him, the way he could tell her anything, could admit anything and still be loved...

The way he loved her.

He loved her.

His skin felt tight, his blood too hot, as if the words might explode out of him at any moment, right there in the middle of the wedding photos.

He was so crazily in love with Eloise Miller it might have actually driven him mad. And the thought of leaving without her ever knowing that...

He knew he should. She deserved better—someone with less scar tissue, fewer war wounds from love. And, whatever he felt, he didn't know if he could do it. Didn't know if he could take that risk and give everything, fall that deep and risk drowning in love.

But suddenly he knew he had to try.

In all the activity of the wedding day it was easy enough for Eloise to avoid spending any quality time with Noah—especially since Laurel had kindly switched around the place settings so that she didn't have to sit next to him at the top table. But, despite managing to keep her distance, she spent the whole day dreading what was still to come.

The moment she had to get out on the dance floor with Noah.

Had the wedding been anyone's except Melissa's she'd have begged for mercy from the bride, or come up with some excuse. But Eloise refused to let Melissa know just how much she didn't want to be out there, dancing with Noah.

How was she supposed to concentrate on the steps when his arms were around her? How could she stand all those people staring at her, watching them together, thinking they already knew all their secrets?

But, one way or another, she'd have to get through it. Then tomorrow he'd be on a plane, flying away from her, and it would all be over.

She bit the inside of her cheek to stop the tears. That was supposed to be a comforting thought.

Eventually, she'd pushed her food around her plate so many times that everyone else had finished eating. She managed to excuse herself during the speeches, to go and check that the ballroom was ready for the evening reception, so she didn't have to hear Noah wax lyrical about the sort of love he didn't believe he was capable of. That might have driven her over the edge.

'Nearly there,' Laurel said as she led the guests—laughing and more than a little tipsy—through to the ballroom a short time later. 'Just get through the dancing and it's all over. I'll deal with the rest from there. Okay?'

Eloise nodded. 'Thanks.'

Laurel's response was a fierce hug. 'We can't let them break us. Whatever they do. We're stronger than that.'

'I know,' Eloise said. She just wished she believed it in her heart as well as in her head.

Before she had time to think of escaping, the Master of Ceremonies was announcing the first dance and Melissa and Riley took to the floor. Eloise watched them spin elegantly around the room and waited for Noah to approach, steeling herself for his touch again.

'May I have this dance?' She spun to find him standing behind her, his hand outstretched, and gave a sharp nod as she took it. All business—

that was the key. This was part of her job…that was all.

Except…

Noah pulled her into his arms as he led her onto the dance floor and she focused on a point over his left shoulder just so she didn't have to look into his eyes and see what was missing there. See again how wrong she'd been to think this could be anything more than a fling.

'Eloise,' he murmured, and she felt his voice all the way through her body. 'Look at me. Please.'

She didn't want to. But she couldn't resist the need in his voice. Setting her jaw, she turned her head, just enough to meet his gaze—and promptly stumbled over her own feet at what she saw there.

Noah caught her, kept them moving, but Eloise wasn't concentrating on the dance any longer.

She was watching his eyes, and feeling the depth of the emotion radiating from them.

'You were right,' he said, as the dance continued. 'I've been wanting to tell you all day, almost since the moment I saw you walking down the aisle towards me, and I realised. I don't want to be safe—not if it means I can't have you. I want more. I want love, and I'm willing to take the risk to get it.'

They were the words she'd been waiting for, but Eloise couldn't trust them, not yet. 'You say the right thing for a living, Noah. Why should I believe you this time over all the things you said this morning?'

'Because I was an idiot. Because…because I was so scared of losing you I couldn't let myself close enough in the first place. But I realised something today. Losing you might destroy me, but no more than letting you go without even giving this a try would. I should have known last night, when I lied to that reporter about what you meant to me. I wanted to tell a different lie, you know. To tell her that it was serious, that we were together—because that would have got me the role I wanted so badly. I told you, I promised the director no flings. But if I'd told them this was a real relationship, I might have got away with it.'

'But you didn't,' Eloise said, confused. Why hadn't he? He wanted that part desperately; she knew that. So why not take the easy way out? 'Why not?'

'Because I was trying to protect you, crazy as

that sounds. So I gave up the part for you—and I ended up hurting you even more. I'm so sorry, Eloise.' He pulled her closer, so close that his lips could touch hers if she just moved an inch. But she stayed motionless, wanting to hear every last word he had to say. 'But I promise you, this isn't an act. It's not a part I'm playing, I swear. It's just me, putting my heart on the line for what I hope is the last time. And I'll take that risk every single day if I have to, if it means you'll keep on loving me as much as I love you.'

The music had stopped, she realised belatedly. They weren't dancing any more; they were just standing in the centre of the dance floor, so wrapped up in each other she couldn't see anything else. But she knew what was happening.

Everyone was watching them. The guests, Melissa, Laurel, Sara the journalist and her photographer…everyone. And, whatever happened next, it would be recorded for posterity on the Internet, she was sure.

And she didn't care. Not one bit.

Because Noah was letting his walls down at last, and she was there to walk right in.

She smiled and his whole body sagged with relief as he gathered her close and kissed her, long and hard and deep.

'This is it, though,' she said, the moment they broke apart. 'You can't shut me out again, once you've let me in.'

'I know. I won't. I won't let you down again.' He kissed her again, swift and soft. 'But…I can't change who I am either. People will be watching us; you know that.'

'Noah, they're watching right now.' She laughed. 'Melissa is going to be furious.'

'I don't care about Melissa. Or any of them. I only care about you.'

'And I'll be fine.' She smiled up at him, certainty running through her veins. 'I wouldn't risk it for anyone else. But for you…I'll stand in any spotlight you want, as long as you're at my side.'

Because this was for ever. She'd known it from the moment they'd first spent the night together, even if she hadn't let herself admit it until later. And, even if it wasn't, it would still be worth it.

Because this wasn't Hollywood. This was real love.

And Eloise was going to get her happy ever after, after all.

* * *

Noah grabbed Eloise close and kissed her again, trying to put all his love, his relief and his truth into that one kiss. This was right. This was the way things were meant to be, the story he was meant to be a part of.

And thank heavens Eloise was willing to let him.

Eventually, he broke the kiss, keeping Eloise tight in his arms. Around him, the guests had broken into applause, with the odd whoop and cheer, and for once Noah thought he might be the one to blush. But when he looked down at Eloise, her cheeks were their usual pale, creamy white above her perfect smile.

'We should probably take a bow,' she said, amusement in her voice. 'I mean, that was quite a show we just put on there.'

He was pretty sure she was joking, but he pulled away to stand at her side all the same, taking her hand in his and swinging them up as he led them in a bow. Laughter went up around the room, and when he stood straight again he could see Melissa glaring at them. He blew her a kiss. That should annoy her.

'So, Noah, am I right in thinking you might like to amend your statement from last night?' Sara asked, her phone recording as before, and her photographer already taking shots of him and Eloise.

'Yes,' he said. 'I most certainly would.'

Then, turning to stare into Eloise's loving eyes, he said the truest line of his career.

'This isn't a fling. It's for ever.'

Eloise smiled. 'And for ever starts now.'

EPILOGUE

'NOAH! NOAH!'

The reporter yelled across the press area, and Noah pasted on a smile as he turned to answer her questions. The smile became more genuine when he realised it was Sara, the reporter who'd broken the story about him and Eloise.

'Are you pleased with the reception *Eight Days After* has had at the festival?'

Was he pleased? No, he was ecstatic. The film had made its debut at the fringe film festival that afternoon, and already it was the only thing anyone there was talking about.

Of course, if it hadn't been so popular, maybe he'd have been able to escape the interviewers a little earlier and get back to Eloise…

Eloise. Just the thought of her made him smile. Thankfully, Stefan had seen how important she was to him, and realised that having Eloise at his side meant that Noah would be calm, centred and everything he needed to be to give his all to the film.

'I'm thrilled,' he said honestly. 'I think it's an important film, a fantastic script, and it has a real message of hope for viewers. I'm glad that those people who've seen it seem to agree.'

'And that's not the only thing they agree on,' Sara said, looking down at her notepad. 'Consensus across the board is that it's your best performance to date—and that you're going to sweep the board with this one come award season.'

'I can't speak for that,' Noah said modestly, while hoping against hope that she was right. 'I'm just glad I managed to pull it off.'

'And why is that, do you think?' Sara's lips twitched up into a knowing smile. 'Could it be that true love might have inspired you to greatness?'

Noah laughed. 'Inspired me to greatness? I don't know about that. But I do know that I'm late to meet my girlfriend. Today's a big day for her too, you see. So, if you'll excuse me...'

He was already halfway across the room before Sara responded. After all, Eloise was waiting for him. Eighteen months ago he'd sworn that he'd never let her down again. And he intended to keep that promise for the rest of his life.

Eloise checked the set-up one last time, then glanced at her watch. Where was Noah? He'd promised he'd be there on time.

'I'm sorry!' She heard his voice before she saw him, pushing his way past circus performers and a waitress carrying a tray of specially designed festival cocktails. 'I'm here!'

'Just as well,' Eloise said with a smile, as she stepped into Noah's arms for a brief kiss. 'From what I hear, you're the star of the festival.'

'Not me, the film.' Noah stepped back and looked around the outside space she'd commandeered for the opening night party. 'And that's only until they see this place. Wow! This is quite the show you're putting on, honey.'

Eloise shrugged. 'The festival committee said they wanted a spectacle, so that's what I'm giving them.' A garden party complete with entertainment, music, the best canapés on the West Coast, magical lighting and some of the special touches that Eloise's company—Spectacle Events—had become famous for, over the last year and a half.

And what a year and a half it had been. While Noah had thrown himself into his role in *Eight Days After,* she'd focused on pursuing the dreams she'd let fall by the wayside for so long. It was as if having found her way into the spotlight, and with Noah at her side, she suddenly knew she could achieve anything.

The best part, she'd found, was the evenings they spent together at Noah's LA home—her home now too—talking through their day, preparing a meal and eating it together, or just kissing until they fell into bed.

Which wasn't to say there hadn't been difficult moments too—times when one of them was working too many hours, or when Noah retreated back into himself after an emotional day's filming. But the difference, Eloise had realised, was that now she had the confidence to call him out... and he had the faith and trust in her to let her.

Tonight was the culmination of eighteen months of love, laughter and hard work—for both of them. Spectacle Events had started small, with just Eloise and her clipboard organising baby showers and birthday parties, but it had grown as word got around. She wasn't naive enough any more to believe that some of that word of mouth didn't have something to do with her being Noah Cross's girlfriend—but she also knew she wouldn't have landed the jobs she had, or been able to expand into real offices with an actual staff, if she wasn't good at what she did.

She was proud of herself—and even prouder of Noah. She'd watched the film the night before, with Stefan the director and the rest of the cast, rapt as Noah nailed every emotion, every moment of pain or guilt his character felt. She'd squeezed his hand tight at the most emotional parts, and known that he'd be offered any part he wanted after this performance.

'I couldn't have done it without you,' he'd murmured as the credits rolled.

And now, tonight, it was her turn to shine. To show Hollywood what she was capable of.

And she was nervous as anything.

'I'm so glad you're here,' she said, reaching out to take Noah's hand again.

'I wouldn't be anywhere else.' Noah tugged her close, back into his arms. 'Especially as I have something I need to ask you. Before the world and his wife descend on this shindig of yours.'

'Oh? What's that?' Eloise asked, glancing away towards the entrance. Was that the first group of reporters and guests arriving?

When she looked back, Noah was down on one knee, and her eyes widened.

'Eloise Miller...' Noah started.

'Is he proposing?' The shout came from the entrance, where one of the waiters was trying to hold back a couple of reporters.

'He was trying to!' Noah yelled back. 'Think you could give us a minute here?'

Eloise shook her head. 'You know they won't. A photo of you down on one knee might be more valuable than the one of us falling out of a cupboard.'

'The world is always watching, huh?'

'Seems like it.'

Noah reached into his pocket and pulled out the most beautiful ring Eloise had ever seen—a large emerald-cut diamond on a platinum band. 'How about you and I really give them something to talk about?'

He pushed the ring onto her finger and Eloise felt a moment of perfect calm settle over her, even in the middle of organising the biggest event of her career, and with the world's media watching.

This. This was exactly where she was meant to be and who she was born to be—and to be with.

She tugged Noah to his feet and wrapped a hand round the back of his head as she pulled him down to kiss her.

'Honey,' she said as they broke the kiss, both breathing heavily. 'They're going to be talking about Noah and Eloise Cross for centuries.'

Noah grinned at her use of his name. 'Oh, yeah? And why's that?'

'Because true love is the best story in the world,' Eloise said, and kissed him again.

* * * * *

*If you loved this book, watch out for
Laurel and Dan's story, coming soon—
the second brilliant book in Sophie Pembroke's
WEDDING OF THE YEAR duet!*

*If you want to treat yourself to another
wedding-themed romance, then try*

*THE PRINCE'S CONVENIENT PROPOSAL
by Barbara Hannay*

MILLS & BOON®
Large Print – May 2017

A Deal for the Di Sione Ring
Jennifer Hayward

The Italian's Pregnant Virgin
Maisey Yates

A Dangerous Taste of Passion
Anne Mather

Bought to Carry His Heir
Jane Porter

Married for the Greek's Convenience
Michelle Smart

Bound by His Desert Diamond
Andie Brock

A Child Claimed by Gold
Rachael Thomas

Her New Year Baby Secret
Jessica Gilmore

Slow Dance with the Best Man
Sophie Pembroke

The Prince's Convenient Proposal
Barbara Hannay

The Tycoon's Reluctant Cinderella
Therese Beharrie

MILLS & BOON®
Large Print – June 2017

The Last Di Sione Claims His Prize
Maisey Yates

Bought to Wear the Billionaire's Ring
Cathy Williams

The Desert King's Blackmailed Bride
Lynne Graham

Bride by Royal Decree
Caitlin Crews

The Consequence of His Vengeance
Jennie Lucas

The Sheikh's Secret Son
Maggie Cox

Acquired by Her Greek Boss
Chantelle Shaw

The Sheikh's Convenient Princess
Liz Fielding

The Unforgettable Spanish Tycoon
Christy McKellen

The Billionaire of Coral Bay
Nikki Logan

Her First-Date Honeymoon
Katrina Cudmore

0517 Rom LP